Dedication

In memory of Coral, an affectionate and loyal little rat terrier.

Coral was found in the streets, starving and afraid of her own shadow. One lucky day soon after, she was adopted by a kind and caring young man who doted on her. Many years later, Coral found him a wonderful wife and gained a loving mother. As the family grew, Coral became a good and protective big sister to two precious little girls.

Coral enjoyed a long and happy life with her human family. Then, on a cold January day, she peacefully fell asleep in her father's arms in front of the fireplace.

"You are missed and will be forever remembered, my furry grandbaby."

Red in the Snow

J. S. Marlo

Print ISBNs
Amazon print 9780228635925
Ingram Spark 9780228635932
Barnes & Noble 9780228635949
BWL Print 9780228635956

BWL Publishing Inc.

Books we love to write ...
Authors around the world.

http://bwlpublishing.ca

Table of Contents

Chapter 1

Raven Brook rode her snowmobile through the forest, swerving left and right between trees laden with snow.

Searching for a three-legged German Shepherd at dawn when a snowstorm loomed on the horizon was insane. Every bone in her body agreed, but her heart refused to listen to reason. She couldn't let Rusty freeze in the bitter January cold. The dog meant everything to her and her son.

The headlights of her snowmobile illuminated the paw prints in the untouched snow.

Rusty liked to chase after squirrels, grouse, and rabbits around the cabin, but she always came back when summoned. Raven couldn't guess what had possessed her dog to run into the forest after peeing near her favourite bush.

Twigs and branches scratched Raven's parka. She risked a glance over her shoulder. Behind her, her son was harnessed to the seat. The tainted visor of his yellow helmet was down, hiding his expression.

Eja should be eating breakfast in his

pajamas, not riding with her all bundled up in his snowsuit, but Raven couldn't leave him alone in the cabin. They only had each other. And Rusty.

The wind picked up, prickling the exposed flesh around Raven's mouth. The leafless trees shivered and the evergreens flapped their branches. Powdery snow swirled in the air, lowering visibility and erasing the paw prints.

A clearing where she often took Eja picnicking in the summer opened ahead. She crossed it, then followed a sinuous path to an old log bridge. No one knew who built it over the stream, but it had withstood years of abuse at the hands of Mother Nature. Until now.

The post and the handrail on the right side were broken.

Raven stopped near the bridge, and keeping the engine running, she disembarked. "You stay here, munchkin. I'll be right back."

Eja bobbed his head. At four years old, he could be trusted to follow her instructions.

She approached the frozen stream on foot. "Rusty!"

There was a ledge under the platform where birds nested, the perfect nook for an animal to crawl into and weather the coming storm. Raven peered under the bridge. Next to the opposite pillar, a ski protruded from the snow.

"How on earth did a snowmobile land in the stream with its ski up?" No one could speed along that path without losing control. Not even her. If anyone tried, they would hit a tree long before they smash into the bridge. "And how did you manage to ram into that post with enough force to break it?"

Bewildered by how the accident could have happened, she trudged down to look under the bridge. To her disappointment, her dog hadn't sought refuge on the ledge.

Raven's gaze travelled back to the ski, and a morbid thought entered her mind.

Cursing her suspicious mind, she ventured onto the frozen stream, and once she reached the ski, she started digging. Within a few sweeps, she exposed a second ski and the hood of the snowmobile.

"Why do I have a bad feeling about this..."

She scooped the snow by the armload, baring a shattered windshield, then a black helmet. At the sight of the red maple leaf painted on its side, her heart somersaulted.

"No... It can't be..."

After a few seconds of hesitation, she brushed the snow off the visor. It was cracked. With a trembling hand, she lifted the visor to get a better view of the rider.

The shock of seeing his lifeless blue eyes and the blood frozen on his face silenced the scream roaring inside her chest.

* * *

Landon Steele reported for duty at the remote Royal Canadian Mounted Police detachment in Sprucetown, Newfoundland.

His new superior officer, Sergeant Cliff Beck, welcomed him with a guttural laugh. "They posted you here after you were caught sleeping in your car while on patrol? That sounds like a cruel and unjust punishment for me."

"I wasn't sleeping." Though Landon had only arrived last night, it sounded like his arguable past had already caught up with him. "I was resting my eyes."

"If you say so. Now listen, Steele." If the glare in Beck's eyes could kill, he wouldn't need the gun attached to his belt. "I'm three months away from retirement. Three. You cause me any trouble, and you'll wish they'd shipped you north. Understood?"

I wouldn't mind being shipped north. One of his buddies had spent a year in Nunavut and enjoyed every second of it. "Got it, Sarge."

"The keys to the building, the garage, and your vehicles are in your drawer." Standing in the doorway of a private office, Beck pointed at a desk underneath a frosty window. "The rear entrance has a keyless entry pad. It's rarely used and must remain locked at all times. The code changes every week, so check your email. Any questions?"

"No questions." Asking why the back door was equipped with a different lock system than the front door would serve no other purpose than indulging Landon's curiosity. Someone had probably decided it wasn't worth spending any money upgrading a building set to be demolished in a few years. The detachment was a relic from the sixties. The construction of a new building had been approved, and the project was scheduled to break ground this coming spring.

"Good." Beck donned his winter jacket. "Try to stay awake long enough to close the files on your desk. And remember, you're on call twenty-four-seven."

Yeah, I know... In small detachments, resources were limited, and the officers were on permanent standby for the duration of their posting.

A mountain of paperwork was piled on his new desk. Landon grabbed the closest folder and looked inside.

Five drunken men arrested for disorderly conduct.

The report dated back to November 10th. The arresting officer, Corporal Gage Harrison, went missing two weeks later, but his frozen body wasn't found until January 15th. Landon didn't mind picking up where Harrison had left off, but that report should have been filed long ago. "Sarge? These arrests took place three months ago."

"That's called backlog, Steele. This is supposed to be a six-person detachment, but I was already short one officer when Harrison went missing. Now Mathis is gone on mat leave, Edwards is on extended vacation, God knows where, and Harrison ain't coming back. That leaves Constable Tobin, me, and behold, *you*." Beck headed for the front entrance. "If there's an emergency, I'll be at Alessi Harrison's. She needs my help finalizing the arrangements for her husband's funeral tomorrow."

Landon didn't see or hear anyone else in the detachment. "Is there a clerk answering the phone or manning the front counter?"

"She quit last week. She was tired of dealing with complaints, so she went to work at the mine for twice the pay and half the aggravation. If you hear of anyone looking for a job, get them to apply. In the meantime, I assume you know how to answer a phone or greet a visitor." His sergeant opened the door. "Make sure you lock the front door if you step out and there's no one else inside."

A draft of frigid air blew over the unmanned counter separating the unsecured work area from the lobby, chilling Landon to the bones.

Alone in the detachment, he tossed the report back on his desk and wandered around.

A curling trophy engraved with Tobin's

name rested on the corner of the uncluttered desk next to Landon's.

"You're either very efficient, Tobin, or very adept at dodging assignments. I can't *wait* to meet you."

A brightly lit corridor marked by closed doors on each side led to unlocked and empty jail cells.

Landon had heard of the working and living conditions in remote communities, but if someone had told him last week that he would be posted here, he would have laughed.

* * *

Not in a mood to eat breakfast, or anything else, Raven poured herself another cup of black coffee, then leaned against the kitchen counter.

In another lifetime, she might have attended the funeral, but not under the current circumstances. Finding his body was bad enough. She didn't need to see him lying in a coffin.

Seated at the kitchen table, Eja dropped his spoon in his bowl, splashing oatmeal on his pajama top and scaring off Rusty, who dashed out of the room.

"Is it still too hot?" Raven had already put his bowl in the freezer for a few minutes. "Want me to cool it some more?"

Her son knocked into thin air. Three times. His own silent signal for *someone's at the door.*

"I'll go answer. Just keep eating." Without waiting for an acknowledgment, she crossed into the living room.

Rusty scratched at the door, her tail wagging to the left.

"Stand back, Rusty." Raven nudged the animal aside with her knee and opened the door.

A front of frigid air swept inside the cabin at the sight of her visitor.

"Hello, Raven."

"Tobin?" At the best of times, the constable's visits were an inconvenience she tolerated. Today, she had no patience to spare for the cocky officer.

With his curly strawberry blond hair, disarming smile, and strapping physique, Tobin could have been a poster boy for model agencies. Unfortunately for him, she was immune to his charms.

Her dog showed her teeth and growled.

"The beast doesn't like me, does he?" Tobin voiced his usual greeting at the same time he stomped one boot on the floor.

Rusty jumped back and retreated to the couch, her tail between her two hind legs.

"No, she doesn't." Raven wanted to rebuke Tobin for scaring her dog, but the message would either fly over his head, like Rusty's gender, or he would take it as an invitation to further ill-treat her scaredy dog.

"What do you want?"

"I'm attending a colleague's funeral in a few hours. Why don't you send the boy and his beast to his room and show some compassion?" He took a step inside and unzipped his jacket. His hand lingered on his shiny belt buckle. "Checking on you every week isn't part of my job description. I deserve some kind of compensation on a day like this."

His gall sickened her. As much as she fantasized chopping off one of his appendages or reporting him for sexual harassment, she couldn't. Tobin would claim she had misread his lips.

The words of a supposedly respected RCMP officer would outweigh the words of a hearing-impaired indigenous woman rumoured to have been arrested for prostitution. Speaking up against Tobin would only further tarnish her reputation. "I have a better idea, Tobin. Why don't you stop checking on me and get out? I would hate to mistake you for a bear and shoot you."

The officer stared her down. "You live alone in the forest, Raven. Don't push your luck."

* * *

Landon had been morally obligated to attend Gage Harrison's funeral, but the reports waiting on his desk gave him a good excuse to skip the reception hosted by his widow.

However, before driving back to the detachment, he made a detour by Dr. Caleb Marshall's Medical Clinic.

In the morgue located in the basement of Marshall's clinic, a man in his early thirties mopped the floor. His ginger ponytail swayed across his back with each sweep.

Landon unzipped his winter jacket. "Hey, there."

The man leaned on his mop. "Hello, Officer. What can I do for you?"

"Sorry to disturb you, but I'm looking for Dr. Marshall." From what Landon had gathered, the town doctor was also in charge of the morgue and acted as medical examiner on special occasions. "I checked upstairs. He's not on duty at the clinic. He wouldn't be around, would he?"

"I'm Marshall, but everyone calls me Caleb or Doc." Amusement wrinkled the corners of Caleb's piercing ebony eyes. "I'm always on duty, one way or another."

I know that feeling. "I'm Corporal Landon Steele. I was told you kept Corporal Gage Harrison's body in a refrigerated bay down here for a few days before you sent him to a top facility in St. John's where an autopsy was performed."

"Yes. Your guys were able to extricate him and bring him here before a blizzard isolated the town for two days. I figured the

RCMP would open an investigation into one of their own regardless of my findings, so I signed his death certificate, kept him frozen, and shipped him as soon as the roads reopened." The doctor had insured Harrison's body was given all the attention it had deserved. "My sister, Raven Brook, was the one who found his body. May I ask if the investigation is over?"

"The medical examiner concluded Harrison died from blunt force trauma following a violent vehicular accident." Landon had seen the pictures taken from the crash site. It appeared unlikely Harrison would have survived the accident even if he had been rescued right away. "Based on what you know of Harrison and what you saw when he was brought in, do you agree with her conclusion?"

"You're here because I phoned your detective Kinley about the autopsy report, aren't you?" Caleb chucked the mop in the corner, between a bucket and a wheeled cart. "The kind of injuries your officer sustained are usually the result of a violent crash or a vicious beating. In Harrison's case, it was obvious he'd crashed to his death. So yes, I agree with your medical examiner's conclusion, but when I saw her note about a four-centimetre-long wound in the fat tissue of his left hand below his thumb, it got me thinking about an incident that happened three days before Harrison's wife reported him missing."

Landon pulled a stool from under the autopsy table and sat. "Keep going, Doc. You have my full attention."

"Back in November, on a quiet Sunday evening, Harrison called me at home. He wanted to know if he needed a tetanus shot because he'd just cut himself with a kitchen knife. I checked his medical record and told him he didn't need a booster. In any case, I told him to meet me at the clinic in half an hour if what he described as a nasty cut to his left hand didn't stop bleeding. He never showed up. His wife Alessi reported him missing three days later. No one heard from Harrison for a full week, then out of the blue, he resurfaced the following Wednesday evening at a strip club in Rocky Cliff, an hour north of here." The doctor began pacing the morgue. "I've known Harrison since he was posted here six years ago. I'm his family doctor and I can't begin to explain his aberrant behaviour, but that's beside the point."

"This is off the record, Doc. Feel free to add any comments you want." In order to understand what happened to Harrison, Landon felt he needed to know the man under the uniform. "I'm in no rush."

"Your medical examiner didn't list any other or previous injuries to his left hand." Caleb's gaze wandered to the round clock hung on the wall above a glass cabinet displaying bones, skulls, and strange specimens in transparent jars. "I thought your detective would want to know about Harrison's nasty Sunday cut since your medical examiner estimated the wound to be two to four days old."

The timeline jumped at Landon. "You think the *fresh* wound mentioned in the autopsy report is the same as the nasty cut Harrison called you upon ten days before he was seen at the strip club?"

"I don't know, but I wish Harrison had come to the clinic. If the cut was as nasty as he claimed, it should have left an obvious scar, and if this is indeed the wound listed in the autopsy report, then Harrison died around the time his wife reported him missing. He couldn't have hooked up with that stripper a week later, not that I have any evidence to support my suspicions." Caleb paused by the counter and opened a drawer from which he retrieved a small yellow mitten with black polka dots. "His daughter's mitt fell from his coat pocket when he was transported in the morgue. I was told to give it back to his widow, but what am I supposed to tell her? *Here's Lyn's mitten. Gage had it with him when he hooked up with a stripper and died.* In her place, I'm not sure I'd want it back. Besides, I'm sure Alessi already bought little Lyn a new pair."

"Just keep it in a drawer for the time being." Landon saw no urgency in ever returning the mitten. "According to the tox screen, Harrison's blood alcohol content was

0.23, nearly three times the legal limit for driving. Would he have been in any condition to drive a snowmobile?"

Caleb couched up a chuckle. "At that level, he would have experienced blackouts. He would have been in no shape to operate any vehicle. I'm amazed he was able to stay on his seat long enough to crash."

That makes two of us, Doc.

* * *

Eager to go to bed, and forget she missed his funeral, Raven switched off the porch lantern powered by a propane generator.

Darkness reclaimed the clearing where her grandfather built the log cabin half a century ago.

In the silence of the night, the flames dancing in the brick fireplace cast fiery shadows on the dark windows. She added another log to the hearth, one of many she would throw in throughout the night to keep the fire burning. With the cabin warm and cozy, she entered Eja's room.

Her son slept with his door open and a grey koala bear in his arms.

She pulled the blankets tight around his small body. "Sweet dreams, munchkin."

Lying on top the blanket near Eja's feet, Rusty pricked an ear.

"Good night, Rusty." It still boggled

Raven's mind to recall that Rusty had been waiting on the front porch upon their return from the bridge. The paw prints in the snow had led to Gage's body—paw prints that Raven had believed belonged to her dog—but now, she wasn't so certain.

Her dog jumped off the bed and hurried out of the bedroom. Raven found Rusty scratching at the front door with her lone front paw.

"You need to pee again?" Raven released the latch and pulled the door ajar. Bitter cold swept in, permeating her flannel pajamas. She cringed from the chilling assault. "Hurry, it's freezing outside."

Rusty took a step backward, turned around, and retreated by the fireplace.

"No game, Rusty." Raven's teeth rattled and her skin prickled. "It's too late to play."

Snowflakes swirled onto the doormat. In their midst, a red envelope wafted into the cabin, landing near her woolen slippers.

A lump caught in her throat, and shivers not brought on by the severe weather coursed through her body.

She donned her parka and mukluks, grabbed the loaded hunting rifle stowed on the ledge above the door, and ventured outside.

Chapter 2

Alone at the detachment, Landon stared at his computer. The front door creaked, prompting him to look around the screen.

His younger colleague stepped in with a large bag. "Steele? You're in early."

Coming to work at dawn had given Landon the opportunity to hack into the computer on his desk without anyone peeking over his shoulders. He had been thrilled to realize the hardware had belonged to Harrison. Unfortunately, all the personal files had been deleted. "I have lots of cases to close. What's in the bag?"

"A toy train for Lyn, Alessi's daughter. She's a sweet kid." Tobin tossed his winter jacket on his chair. "She needs a decent father figure in her life."

On his way to the detachment, Landon had made a detour by Tim Hortons. While he waited for his coffee and muffin, he had overheard two patrons gossiping about Tobin and Harrison's widow. Despite Harrison's dishonourable death, duty demanded that fellow officers lend his widow a helping hand. "How's her mother coping?”

“Alessi is an extraordinary woman.” Tobin’s eyes reflected his admiration. “She’s better off without Harrison.”

Landon kept a straight face while silently admonishing himself for not paying more attention to those rumours. “I’ll take your word for it.”

“I’m telling you, Steele, the guy was a scumbag, but Alessi still gave a heart-wrenching eulogy at his funeral. Harrison didn’t deserve her.” The constable stepped into the corridor. “I don’t smell coffee. Did you forget to brew a fresh pot?”

Landon arched a brow. “Making coffee isn’t part of my job description.”

The front door opened. An indigenous woman stepped in and approached the reception counter.

“Hello, Raven.” Tobin paused at the entrance of the corridor. “I’m busy, but our new corporal will take care of you.”

An icy front swept between Tobin and the woman.

Bracing himself for a verbal altercation, Landon proceeded toward the counter, coming face to face with angry, ocean blue eyes. “I’m Corporal Steele, ma’am. How can I help you?”

“I’m being threatened and I’m growing tired of it.” A strange accent lingered in the woman’s voice. She presented him with a red envelope. “Feel free to relate that last part to your sergeant.”

The reason behind her animosity toward Beck wasn't clear. Still, before accepting the envelope, Landon snapped on a pair of disposable gloves.

A white pom-pom brushed the woman's arm. As he took the envelope, Landon peeked over the top of the counter. A blue-eyed child gazed at him with unconcealed curiosity.

"Hi there." When the child didn't respond, Landon turned his attention to the short message tucked inside the envelope.

I'm coming for you, Brook. Pack your Ugly Brat and get out while you can.

The child looked neither ugly nor bratty. Nevertheless, the unveiled threat was too specific to be a random act.

"Where and when did you receive the note, Ms. Brook?" Tobin had called her Raven, so Landon assumed Brook to be her last name. When she didn't immediately correct him, he committed the name to memory, where it superposed with the name provided by Caleb. *You're his sister, the woman who found Harrison's body.*

"I live in a log cabin in the forest, about twenty klicks from here. Around midnight, my dog heard someone at the door. When I answered, the wind carried the envelope inside. It would have been placed on the front porch. There were footprints in the snow. I followed them to the shed where they stopped at the edge of fresh snowmobile tracks.”

“Someone threatens you and you chase after him in the middle of the night?” Landon was stunned she had acted so fearlessly.

“What else was I supposed to do? Call you?” Her nostrils flared. “You didn’t bother showing up for the second or third note, and that’s the fourth one.”

The three previous notes had to predate his posting here, or else he would have heard about them, and while he didn’t appreciate being tossed in the same basket as Tobin and Beck, Landon understood her resentment at being ignored. “Did you follow the snowmobile tracks?”

“In the dark? While my son was asleep?” The dubious look she gave him bordered on contempt. “I’m not stupid, Corporal.”

“Of course not. I didn’t mean to imply anything.” Her restraint somewhat reassured Landon. “I meant this morning in broad daylight, not last night.”

“A storm raged last night.” Long black eyelashes fluttered, casting a shadow over her eyes. “By morning, the wind had erased the prints and tracks.”

“I’ll look into it.” He eased the note back into the envelope. “And keep you posted.”

“Sure...” Her guarded acknowledgement showed little faith in his ability to apprehend the culprit.

She left with her son. The door banged behind them.

The corner of the envelope pinched between his thumb and finger, Landon searched his side of the counter for evidence bags.

Anyone with a basic sense of organization would have placed the bags next to the box of disposable gloves. He turned toward the corridor and was surprised to see Tobin still leaning against the wall. "Do we have any evidence bags anywhere?"

"In the galley." Tobin smirked, heading down the corridor. "You can ditch the gloves. We didn't find any prints on the other notes or envelopes. You won't find any on this one. They're always dropped in the middle of the night during a snowstorm, and there's never any footprints or tracks left by morning. In my opinion, she writes them herself."

Not impressed by the theory, Landon darted a covert look in his colleague's direction while searching the cupboards for bags. "On what exactly are you basing that opinion?"

"The woman is half deaf." Tobin opened a cupboard and then tossed him a box of sealable bags. "Not the brightest star in the sky, if you get my drift."

"No, I don't get your drift." Stunned by the comment, Landon stared at his colleague who had either missed the sensitivity training or slept right through it. *The only person lacking intelligence is you, Tobin. Your prejudice has no place in the organization.* "How does she communicate?"

"She mostly reads lips." Tobin's sneer of disdain mixed with the whooshing of the water as he rinsed the coffee pot. "She understands what she wants to understand. The boy isn't any better than his mother."

Who did you blackmail to get accepted into the RCMP, Tobin? Because you sure didn't earn the privilege of wearing this uniform. Swept by a wave of dismay, Landon strived to remain impassive. "Where are the other notes?"

"Filing cabinet in Beck's office. He shelved her complaints." Tobin placed a new paper filter in the coffee maker. "If I were you, I'd stay away from her. She's trouble."

Good thing I like trouble. "I didn't ask for your opinion, Tobin." Appalled by his colleague's attitude, Landon marched toward his desk.

The door of Beck's office was open, and the light was on. His sergeant was hanging his winter jacket on a hook attached to the wall next to another frosty window.

Landon walked in the office without being invited.

His sergeant raised a disapproving brow. "Ever heard of knocking?"

"No." Rattling Beck's chain served its purpose. "Raven Brook stopped by with another threatening note. Apparently, it wasn't the first one."

"She lives in her grandfather's cabin in the middle of the woods. No one has any reason to threaten her." Beck growled, pulling on the second drawer of a file cabinet. "It should be her somewhere... Here it is." He tossed a folder on the corner of his desk. "Tobin didn't deem the previous threats credible, but feel free to investigate them again."

* * *

On her way to the medical clinic, Raven sighted a RCMP pickup truck. The digits one-zero-three-six were written in navy blue paint on the white tailgate.

Gage's truck. Former truck.

The sergeant drove the biggest SUV in the fleet, and Tobin always showed up behind the wheel of a noisy cruiser. One of them had either switched vehicles, or the truck had been reassigned to that new corporal she had met a week earlier.

With his angular face and piercing brown eyes, Steele had inspired confidence. When she had dropped the note, he had acted like he cared. She should have known better.

The truck was parked behind The Polar Skin, the only strip club in town.

Steele is just like Gage. She should have investigated the threats on her own after receiving the second note instead of hoping someone would take her seriously.

Through the rearview mirror, Eja stared at her with glassy eyes. Not to upset her son, Raven kept her anger at bay, even managing a bittersweet smile. "We're almost there, munchkin."

She parked behind Caleb's clinic, then scooped Eja from his car seat. His head rested against her shoulder and his arms hung loose down his sides. "Uncle Caleb will make you feel better."

A dozen people occupied the waiting room.

"Good morning, Raven." Ayita, Caleb's full-time receptionist, greeted her with a smile. "What can I do for you?"

"Eja woke up with a high fever." Raven didn't have an appointment, not that she needed one. Caleb would wring her neck if she were to drive an hour to get to the nearest hospital instead of coming to see him. Still, she didn't like to cut in line. Other patients needed him too. "I see Caleb is busy, but is there any chance you could squeeze me in today?"

"Follow me." Ayita ushered them into the last room at the end of a short hallway. "Your brother will see you next."

Inside The Polar Skin, patrons gathered around the dancing poles, ready for the first show.

Landon checked his watch. It wasn't even 10 a.m. yet.

After the opening of a new gold mine three years earlier, the town of barely one thousand had seen its population explode. Attracted by high wages, four times as many men as women had moved into Sprucetown. To the chagrin of many longtime residents, crime, disturbance, and adult entertainment had also followed in their wake.

Landon didn't understand the point of moving here to make extra money only to squander it on strippers.

Not here to watch the show, he elbowed his way backstage only to encounter a wall of flesh, bones, and muscles.

"Step aside, Brutus." Bouncers had never intimidated Landon. When they didn't wear any nametags, like the fellow in front of him, Landon nicknamed them Brutus, regardless of their size, age, or race. "I need to have a friendly chat with Whiskey—and she's not worth a battle scar."

At about the same height, but some fifty pounds heavier, the dark-skinned bouncer gauged Landon. A crooked nose and a scar above his left eye added an element of danger to his stance.

The bouncer held his gaze, then without uttering a sound, he stepped sideways. "Last room on the right."

In the last room, two girls in various stages of undress fumbled with their hair and makeup.

While on patrol, Landon had seen Whiskey's name advertised for *One Day Only* on the opaque window of the strip club. Hoping she was the right Whiskey, he had decided to pay her a visit before wasting two hours on a return trip to Rocky Cliff.

"Which one of you is Whiskey?" His money was on the brunette with short, curly hair, but when she hurriedly left the room, Landon was reminded why he never gambled.

The blonde, applying a thick coat of pink lipstick the same shade of gaudy pink as the lacy push-up bra and undies promoting her generous attributes, glanced at him through the mirror. "What do you want, big guy?" She smacked her lips together. "A private show?"

No, not even for free. "Are you the same Whiskey who danced at the Rocky Cliff Bar an hour north?"

"I'm the one and only Whiskey on The Rock." She swayed her hips walking toward him in high-heeled stilettos. "If my reputation is preceding me, the tips will be worth the trip."

The possibility she had come to perform at The Polar Skin so she could capitalize on her new fame—the last woman to have seen Corporal Harrison alive—churned Landon's stomach. "Two weeks ago, you told a detective you hooked up with Corporal Harrison after your show back in November. Tell me about that night again."

"Already told the rude detective everything." She trailed a long, pink fingernail down the front of his uniform. "Why don't you go ask him, big guy?"

Her breath smelled of onion and tobacco.

Landon grabbed her wandering hand by the wrist. "Unless you want to be arrested for solicitation and miss your opening performance, you should talk. Fast."

Defiance burned in her eyes. She took a step back, pulling her hand away. "Back in November, Harrison sat in a dark corner booth at the Rocky Cliff Bar. Alone. He paid five hundred bucks for a table dance."

Harrison couldn't afford a five-hundred-dollar dance, not on a corporal's pay, not when he had to provide for his family. *Not unless he had other revenues.* "For that price, it must have been one heck of a dance."

"He had his cap on. I couldn't really see his expression, but it sure felt like he enjoyed the show." Sweat beaded in the cleft of her breasts. "After my shift, he invited me for a drink. It must have been around two in the morning. I met him in the parking lot. He was waiting for me in his police truck." A sly smile crossed her face, showing yellowed teeth. "I've been arrested before and tossed into the back seat, but it was kind of exciting to be in the front seat. Much more comfortable."

In the front seat of the truck I've been driving all week? Once he got home, Landon would wash the image with a red beer. "He paid you to have sex in the truck?"

"No!" The shrill objection rang like a fingernail scratching a blackboard. "The poor guy was drunk and lonely. He just wanted to talk."

"Talk?" The rumours that Landon had heard suggested otherwise. "And what did you talk about?"

"His miserable life." She browsed through a clothes rack. "He was slurring and not very coherent. He rambled on about not getting a promotion, wanting to move, making less money than the guys working at the mine... he also talked about his wife and little girl, about not letting them down... He kept repeating he should quit, so I told him he should stop drinking and go home. He gave me his badge and drove away."

An officer would never give his badge away. "Was he in uniform?"

"Yes." She held up two short leather skirts. "Should I wear the black or the red?"

Do I look like I care? "Was the ceiling light on in the truck? Did you have a good look at his face?"

"His cap was low over his eyes and he was drinking, but I could still see him, even without the ceiling light on. Besides, he was parked near a lamppost, and the ceiling light turned on when I got in and out. His moustache looked terrible. There was a line where hair didn't grow, but it was him. I'm good at remembering men." She snapped the black skirt around her waist. "When I showed his badge to that detective, he kept it. How do I get it back?"

"Forget the badge." Music overflowed in the room, forcing Landon to raise his voice. "Do you remember if he had an injury or a fresh scar in the palm of his left hand near his thumb?"

"An injury?" She briefly closed her eyes. "He didn't wear gloves and he held his beer can with his left hand. If he was injured, he didn't have any bandage on and it didn't stop him from drinking."

"Whiskey, you're next," a male voice yelled from somewhere outside the room.

She brushed a hip against Landon's thigh. "Am I free to go now, big guy?"

* * *

In the examination room, Raven held Eja's hand while he lay quietly on the table, his mouth wide open.

"I'm suspecting strep throat." Her brother took a swab of Eja's throat. "Has he complained about any pain or discomfort?"

"Not a word." If her son was in pain, he suffered in silence. It broke her heart that she couldn't breach the wall of silence he had built around himself. "But he won't eat or drink."

"I'll run a rapid test just to confirm, but I'm sure it'll come back positive, so do you prefer pills or liquid?"

"Pills." Her son didn't like the taste of the liquid. Feeding him pills was less messy than liquid dripping down his chin, and she didn't have to worry about him getting the full dose.

Caleb scribbled a prescription on his pad and then gave it to her. "Four times a day for the next ten days. If by the end of the week, he hasn't improved, or if he's getting worse, you bring him back, okay?"

Eager to leave and fill the prescription, she nodded.

"Raven?" Caleb touched her forearm, stopping her in her tracks. "It's been three months since he stopped speaking. It's time Eja sees a psychologist."

Knowing her brother was right didn't make the recommendation any easier to swallow. "Could we discuss this another time?"

Caleb smiled, but it didn't erase the concerns etched on his face. "Sure. And don't forget to finish the prescription, even if he starts feeling better."

"I won't. Thanks." On her way out, Raven looked toward the parking lot behind the strip club.

The RCMP truck was gone.

Chapter 3

Alone at the detachment in the wee hours, Landon accessed Detective Kinley's notes regarding Harrison's investigation.

Wednesday morning, November 16th.
Alessi Harrison, his wife, reports him missing when she realizes he never came home after she went to bed.

Wednesday night, November 23rd. A week later.
At 11:09 p.m. Harrison withdraws five hundred dollars from an ATM in Rocky Cliff. The ATM camera shows him in uniform with his jacket unzipped. The nametag on his shirt is visible. His cap rests low on his forehead, obscuring his face, but his moustache, with the gap on the right side, is a match with autopsy photos.

At 11:54 p.m. he uses his credit card to pay for three beers at Strip Bar. He also pays five hundred cash for a table dance.

Wee hours of the morning, Thursday, November 24th.
Around 2 a.m. Harrison drinks in his truck with a stripper named Whiskey, complains about his life, and gives her his badge. She remembers his moustache. Her description matches the autopsy photos.
At 3:37 a.m. Harrison fills up on gas on the outskirt of Rocky Cliff. The camera at the gas station gives a similar photo to the one at the ATM.

Harrison wasn't a heavy drinker and he had a promising future in the RCMP. His uncharacteristic behaviour raises a flag.

Sunday night, November 13th. Prior to all the incidents, Dr. Caleb Marshall receives call from Harrison about an injury he sustained to left hand, but Marshall can't provide any evidence. Wife and officers at detachment don't recall any injury.

The timeline corresponded with Whiskey's account, and the detective had investigated Caleb's phone call. Landon kept reading.

Autopsy photo shows a serious injury to the left hand done two to four days prior to death. No other visible injuries or scars. If this is the injury Dr. Marshall referred to, why would Harrison conceal it from his entourage? The doctor has no reason to lie, which implies Harrison's death could have occurred before his drinking binge in Rocky Cliff, but there's no evidence someone else posed as Harrison in Rocky Cliff. Missing something?

A clear picture of Harrison's face would have removed any doubts regarding his identity. Instead, it had come down to his moustache. A unique moustache, but still only a moustache. Landon continued reading.

Sunday morning,

It bothered Landon that the townspeople had already labelled Harrison a disgraced officer even though the investigation was still on-going.

Unable to provide any answers to Kinley's questions yet, Landon scattered Brook's four threatening notes on his desk.

The first note was dropped on her porch in the middle of the night on Thursday, December 1st.

I'm watching you, Brook.
You don't belong here.

Stalking was a crime, even if the culprit didn't directly threaten her.

The second note was dropped on Tuesday, December 20th.

Playing alone in the forest is dangerous, Deafy. Be careful. Very careful.

The offensive terms suggested the culprit knew she was hearing impaired, though it didn't mean she knew him personally.

The third note was dropped on Wednesday, January 11th.

Bad accidents happen in winter. Beware.

That one resonated like a threat.

The fourth one was dropped on Sunday night, February 5th.

I'm coming for you. Pack your Ugly Brat and get out while you can.

In this last one, Landon perceived a drastic escalation. The culprit had become eager to get rid of her and her son.

Landon still hadn't received the report

from the lab, but he didn't hold much hope for prints or DNA traces, not when the other notes and envelopes had revealed nothing.

The days the envelopes were dropped didn't present any discernible pattern, but on every occasion, a snowstorm had blanketed the town during the night, burying any evidence.

Still, something caught Landon's eye. A curly twist in the loops of the capital *Ps* and *Bs*, present in the words *Playing, Pack, Brook, Be, Bad, Beware,* and *Brat.*

In a court of law, it was called a signature. The culprit had left a signature as distinct as his fingerprints.

Landon needed to pay Raven Brook a visit, to see the cabin and the surrounding area with his own eyes. However, he had hoped for a stronger lead before meeting her again. The realization that he cared about not disappointing her disconcerted him.

The woman lacked faith in the RCMP. His misplaced pride demanded that he redeemed the Mounties' reputation. It had nothing to do with her haunting blue eyes.

The big hand of the clock crept toward twelve as the small hand edged on two. *Time to go home.*

The front door swung open.

The tall, bald man working as bartender at The Polar Skin stepped into the lobby. "There's been an accident at the club, Officer Steele. You need to come right away."

* * *

Raven added another log to the bed of glowing embers. The dry bark combusted instantly.

Memories of cracking and popping sounds resonated in her mind, only to fade under the weight of the responsibilities assailing her.

Eja's fever had lessened its clutch, and he had fallen asleep in her bed with Rusty at his feet.

Back in November, when the nightmares started plaguing his nights, he had sought refuge in her bed. Caught in his imaginary world, he had kicked and pushed until his small body succumbed from exhaustion. For five long weeks, Raven had tried coaxing him back into his own bedroom.

One fateful evening in December, Rusty had jumped onto Eja's bed and waited for him. Her son had reluctantly snuggled next to his dog. From then on, Rusty kept the nightmares at bay, and Raven regained her bedroom.

Nowadays, Eja smiled more, but he still hadn't recovered his voice.

Maybe Caleb is right. Maybe it's time Eja sees a psychologist.

Before settling on the couch with a pillow and a blanket, Raven double-checked that the door was locked.

A small puddle shone on the dark wooden floor where a nick in the weather strip stopped it from flushing smoothly against the sill. She wiped the wet smudge with the cuff of her pajama sleeve.

At the sight of blood staining the white and pink fabric, fear and disgust churned her stomach.

* * *

Behind The Polar Skin, the spotlight above the back door illuminated Landon's disturbing crime scene.

Whiskey's body lay face down in the snow. An icicle poked from her neck, and shards of ice were scattered around her body. More icicles hung from the ledge of the roof, ready to strike.

Crouched by her arm. Landon checked her pulse. No beat or heat emanated from her wrist. *She's dead cold, in more senses than one.*

The air crackled. An icicle grazed his thigh, shattering near his boot. Landon leapt to his feet and moved aside, away from the deadly overhead daggers.

"A customer is fetching Dr. Caleb." The bouncer who had previously attempted to stop Landon from seeing Whiskey knelt on one knee by her chest.

There wasn't much the doctor could do

aside from taking pictures of the body and declaring her dead, but Landon welcomed any insight Caleb might have. "Can you tell me what happened?"

"Whiskey went outside for a smoke around one in the morning. When she didn't show up for her two o'clock show, I looked for her and found her lying in the snow. I called 9-1-1 and sent Baldy to the detachment to relay the message faster."

Faster indeed. The government had implemented a province-wide 9-1-1 service, but Landon had been told the response time wasn't always proportional to the nature of the emergency. "Did you touch her?"

"I checked for pulse and stopped anyone else from approaching her body." Cracks appeared in Brutus's tough demeanour. "Most of the girls don't choose that lifestyle, Officer. Most are forced into it one way or another. Whiskey didn't deserve to die like this."

"I know." Landon wasn't immune to anyone's death or suffering, but he couldn't change the past. His job was to bring justice to the victim and closure to the family. "Now let me see if I get this right. Whiskey went outside with nothing more than a bathrobe and a pair of high-heeled sandals, but no one worried about her disappearance until an hour later?"

The bouncer diverted his gaze toward the side of the building where a red sign banned smoking within three metres of the door. "The girls aren't supposed to smoke near the building, so they often join patrons in their trucks."

Despite the interdiction, cigarette butts littered the snow. The victim didn't pinch any cigarette between her fingers, but it was possible she hadn't lit one yet, or she had dropped it when she was struck by the icicle.

Since Whiskey wasn't dressed for the weather, it's highly probable she had either planned to go somewhere warmer or hadn't intended to step out for more than a few puffs. "Do you know if she was meeting a patron for a smoke?"

"The regular girls know they can trust me with their whereabouts, but it was Whiskey's first time at The Polar Skin." Brutus looked him in the eyes. "If she had plans, she didn't share them with me."

Whiskey's death, less than sixteen hours after Landon interviewed her, didn't sit well with him.

* * *

Rusty unrelentingly scratched at the door.

The constant movement visible in the corner of her eye distracted Raven from her work. This evaluation report was due in a few days. She needed to finish it.

"Do you need to go out, or is there

someone outside?" From the windows, she couldn't see if someone stood in front of the door any more than she could tell if a vehicle was parked on the other side of the shed. *When Gramp built the cabin, he didn't put much thought into the location of the windows.*

Considering Rusty had already ventured outside twice this morning, Raven suspected the presence of a visitor. An unwelcome visitor. She traded her laptop for a loaded rifle, unlocked the deadbolt, and slid the latch.

Aiming at the door, she took a few steps back and flicked the safety pin off. "I'm armed. Come in. Slowly."

The door opened.

Rusty jumped on the visitor and nuzzled him.

"Good morning to you too, big—" Steele gazed in Raven's direction with widening brown eyes. The words died on his lips.

Rusty ran across the room, her tail wagging like a windmill, picked up her octopus fetch toy from her basket, and ran back to the door, dropping it at Steele's feet.

Stumped by her behaviour, Raven gaped in surprise. Rusty was an excellent judge of character, but after the explosion, she had become leery of strangers and terrified of loud noises.

Steele straightened up, and though exhaustion marred his face, he looked ready to pounce or draw his own gun.

It took Raven a few seconds to realize his lips had started moving again. "What did you say?"

"Put the rifle down, please." He articulated clearly, and she imagined his voice carrying through the cabin, deep and rich. "I got shot once. If it's the same to you, I'd rather not repeat the experience."

Caught off guard by his lack of arrogance, she lowered her weapon. "Come in and close the door. It's cold out."

Once inside, he crouched down to play tug-of-war with her dog, Rusty pulling on a tentacle and the officer holding the octopus's head.

Trusting Rusty's instincts, Raven returned the rifle to the ledge. "My son is sleeping. I'd appreciate it if you kept Rusty from barking."

"Rusty?" As soon as his lips began moving, Steele tilted his head up. He had undoubtedly been made aware of her hearing loss. "Interesting name for a vigorous three-legged dog. How did he..." The officer peeked sideways at Rusty's underbelly. "How did she lose a forelimb?"

Few men had ever shown genuine interest toward her dog. Therefore, Raven had only shared Rusty's real story with one of them.

Touched by the effort that Steele made to ascertain her dog's gender, Raven lowered her guard another notch. "Rusty wasn't mine when..." The shockwave, the oily smell in the air, and the destruction still haunted her, but she learned to cope with the memories of that night. Her dog, however, still struggled five years later. "Her paw was crushed, and the vet had to amputate. Pixie was her puppy name but her hand… her owner renamed her Rusty after the red streaks in her black coat. When he could no longer take care of her, I gave her a new home."

She and Rusty were broken. Gramp had understood they needed a safe place to heal, and he had welcomed them with open arms. The cabin, however, didn't offer the safe haven that Raven had hoped for.

"She's beautiful and lucky to have you." Steele cast an admiring gaze on Rusty while playing with her. "How's your son, Raven? Is he hurt?"

Puzzled by the use of her given name, Raven watched their game. "Eja has strep throat and he's feverish, but he's getting better." Her brother could be overprotective at times, but surely Caleb hadn't sent an officer to monitor Eja's recovery. "Why?"

"I saw blood in the snow. It trails from your shed to the house. When you answered with a rifle, I thought something might have happened." The ghost of a smile softened Steele's chiseled face. "By the way, pointing a gun at an officer is never a good idea."

A fire she had extinguished long ago sparked embers in her belly. She hastened to extinguish them. Being lonely wasn't a valid excuse for being foolish. Besides, inquiring about blood was a far cry from caring. "I had another visitor last night."

Steele let go of the octopus and stood. "Another threatening note?"

Rusty retreated with her toy in front of the couch.

"Not a note. A fox." The officer's brows shot up, and Raven chuckled at the dubious look he gave her. "At least I can do something with a dead mammal. Let me check on my son, then I'll show you."

Her dog followed her into Eja's bedroom. Her son was fast asleep. "You stay with Eja." Rusty lay near the bed, her head held high and her ears pricked. "I'll be right back."

Once she geared up, she invited Steele to follow her outside, leading him to the back of the shed. He towered over her by a head, but unlike Tobin, Steele didn't look down at her.

"What brought you here this morning, Corporal Steele?"

"I wanted to ask you a few questions about the threatening notes." He paused within arm's reach of the fox hung to a nail by its hind legs. "Someone left you a bloody carcass? Has that ever happened before?"

I wish. The rusty red fur was gorgeous and worth good money, not that she intended to sell it. "Never. Rusty scratched at the door around two-thirty last night. When I checked outside, I found the fox on the doorstep. I threw it in the snow and cleaned the mess." While Eja had seen many dead animals in his short life, their blood didn't belong on the porch or the floor. "To be honest, I'm surprised the fox didn't vanish. I was expecting whoever tried to scare me to come back and pick it up."

Steele slowly nodded. "Someone wants you gone. Any idea why?"

Over the winter, one reason had crossed her mind, but it couldn't be. No one was aware of her secret, not even Caleb. "I live alone with my son. I'm no threat to anyone, Officer Steele."

"Please, call me Landon."

The request sent strange vibrations through her body. "Landon," she said tentatively. "Am I pronouncing it right?"

He nodded. "You have a lovely voice. I cannot begin to imagine the mental discipline it takes you to read my lips so efficiently."

The lack of sleep, combined with Eja's illness and the discovery of the dead fox, had taken its toll. The compliment breached her defences and struck the wall she had erected around her heart. A few cracks appeared, but to her relief, the wall withstood the assault.

"Unlike what some people think, I don't just read lips. I also rely on the speech sounds I can still hear, on facial expression, body language, gesture, context..." Lip-reading was an art as much as a skill. "I may not get every single word, but during a one-on-one conversation, I never misinterpret the meaning of a sentence." Trying to follow more than one conversation at a time in a loud setting or the middle of a crowd was another story.

"Now I'm even more impressed." He smiled grabbing the fox's paw. "May I take the fox?"

"Why?" She had planned on skinning it and tanning the hide to make moccasins for Eja, like Gramp had taught her.

"If I can determine how the animal was killed, it may give me a lead."

"The left forelimb shows tissue damage and the skull is crushed." The injury suggested the fox had been caught in a leghold trap similar to the ones used by her grandfather. "I'd say it was trapped alive then clubbed to death."

"So I'm looking for a trapper?" His eyes narrowed, making the sentence look more like a question than a statement.

"There are three kinds of trappers around here, Landon. The ones that trap with a permit, the ones that trap without a permit, and the ones that steal other trappers' catches." Raven hadn't trapped since she was a teenager, and she never stole from others, but these three categories encompassed most of the local population of Sprucetown. "Good luck finding the culprit."

He let go of the animal. "We didn't get any snow last night. It's possible he left a trail this time. Would you mind if I look around?"

Despite the brave composure that Raven

strived to maintain, the culprit's increased boldness worried her. "You're really taking the threats against me seriously?"

A gleam of hurt flickered in Landon's eyes, rekindling her silly hope that someone cared. "Yes. Would there be a safe place where you and Eja could stay until I get to the bottom of this?"

"This is my home." Once Caleb learned about the fox, he was bound to insist she and Eja come live with him, but he already shared his house with Annette, his vain girlfriend who was immersed in an online computer science class. *Eja and I aren't his responsibility.* "I'm not leaving my cabin."

Chapter 4

Landon entered the basement of Caleb's clinic. "Hello, Doc."

"Good afternoon, Steele." Caleb looked too jovial for someone interacting with corpses. "I was wondering when I'd see you again."

The stripper lying naked on the stainless-steel table died more than twelve hours ago. Her body should have revealed some answers by now, and Landon was eager to hear them. "What can you tell me about Whiskey?"

"She died of a stab wound to the neck." The doctor washed his hands. "The wound matched the shape of an icicle, but I'm afraid your murder weapon melted."

Landon sighed, exhaling his frustration. "Tell me something I don't know."

The doctor slipped on a pair of disposable gloves and then rolled the cadaver sideways. "Point of entry is here." He pointed a finger at a hole surrounded by bluish skin. "The angle is consistent with an icicle dropping from the roof as she bowed her head."

The timing of her demise bothered Landon. "You're telling me she went for a smoke at the wrong place and time?"

"The stains on her teeth and fingers indicate she was a heavy smoker. There was also half a pack of cigarettes and a lighter in the pocket of her robe." Caleb repositioned Whiskey on her back and covered her with a white sheet. "Smoking outside killed her."

It doesn't mean it was accidental. "Is it possible someone sneaked up from behind and stabbed her with an icicle?" Murdering someone with an icicle sounded ludicrous, but Landon had heard of weirder murder weapons.

The doctor snapped his gloves off. "Anything is possible, but I didn't find any defensive wounds, bruises, scratches, signs of struggle or sexual activity in the hours preceding her death. From a medical point of view, nothing suggests murder."

But nothing rules it out either. "Tox screen?"

"I sent it to the lab. I'll know in a week or so, but I wouldn't pin any hope on the results. Even if she tests positive, the drugs are unlikely to have caused her death. If anything, the presence of illegal substances may have dulled her reflexes, preventing her from quickly stepping aside when, or if, she heard the icicle breaking from the ledge. Would you like me to send her to St. John's for a full autopsy?"

"No, that won't be necessary." An

autopsy wouldn't reveal if she was murdered, but if the owner of the bar had installed a camera at the back, it might have revealed a person of interest. "The other day, you told me your sister found Harrison's body." Landon suspected the fox to be linked to the threatening notes. A glimpse into Raven's life might shed some light over her current predicament. "Could you tell me more about her life?"

"Raven and I aren't blood-related, but we grew up together in the shabby apartment our mothers shared in Toronto. When we were young, they locked us inside a small bedroom for hours with growling stomachs while men came and went. You could say business was booming." Resentment had crept in his voice. "I was a few years older than Raven, so I read her stories to muffle the sounds coming from the next room. When she was seven, her mother died of an overdose. No one came to take her away, so my mother kept her.

"Some months later, my maternal grandfather found us. He wanted my mother to come home and start over, but she refused. That was the last time I saw her. Gramp took Raven and me with him." A faraway look crossed his ebony eyes. "She wasn't his granddaughter, but Gramp couldn't leave her behind. He raised us together in the cabin and made sure we received a proper education. Without him, I'd probably be selling drugs, and Raven would be turning tricks. Instead, I became a doctor, and she became a social worker, but life wasn't easy for her. She got measles when she was eight and suffered damage to both ears. Our mothers hadn't bothered with vaccination. Hearing aids gave her terrible headaches, so she had to learn new skills to cope and succeed."

"Your sister developed impressive communication skills, Doc. Do you know if she encountered any problems at work?" Threats and violence plagued her profession. Landon made a mental note to look into her caseload. "A deadbeat parent holding a grudge?"

"You'll have to ask her. Raven is the strongest advocate for children you'll ever find. She may have a hard time hearing, but she's great at listening." Caleb's distinction between hearing and listening struck a chord. "When Gramp got ill, she came back to take care of him."

Their grandfather would have been proud of both children for rising above the unfortunate circumstances surrounding their births. "Does your grandfather still live in the area?"

"He died five years ago, killed by two teenagers high on drugs. Raven was the one who found his body in the forest." Caleb stared at the dead stripper. "I know we need social workers in this town. I just never expected Raven would give up her career in Halifax to settle down in Gramp's cabin—or give birth to Eja later that year."

Nowhere in the story did Caleb mention a boyfriend, but Landon couldn't rule out the possibility of a former lover seeking revenge. "May I ask who's Eja's father?"

The doctor met Landon's gaze. "No idea. Raven never told me."

* * *

Back at the detachment, Landon leaned in his chair, thinking. *Why a dead fox?*

"Steele!" Beck marched toward his desk and then slammed a report on its corner. "Suspicious death? How much sleep did you get last night?"

Way too little. At this rate, Landon would indeed fall asleep on the job. "Is there a problem, Sarge?"

His sergeant's face swelled like a red birthday balloon. "You have no motive, no murder weapon, no witness, no defensive marks, no nothing. The stripper's death was nothing more than a freak accident."

"She was killed by an icicle. Doesn't that enter the suspicious category?" Pressing Beck's buttons and having fun witnessing his reaction was a perk Landon hadn't anticipated.

"Didn't I tell you not to rock the boat?" Beck gripped the side of his desk, leaning forward, and his breath expelled a sample of his garlicky lunch. "There's enough work to do around here without chasing after imaginary murderers. Got it?"

While Landon might have to accept Whiskey's death was indeed an unfortunate accident, he took the threats against Raven seriously, and so should his sergeant. "Got it, but I was at Raven Brook's cabin this morning. Someone abandoned a dead fox on her porch last night. I couldn't see any suspicious tracks, but they could be mangled with Raven's. There were lots of snowmobile tracks around her—"

"A fox? In case you haven't noticed, Steele, Brook is an indigenous woman. Trapping is in her blood." Visibly exasperated, Beck pulled away from the desk. "Go ahead and investigate her claims, but think twice before risking your career for women like Whiskey or Brook. I would hate to see you end up like Harrison."

How nice of you to care about me or my career. "What do you mean by women like them?"

"Karma has no menu, Steele. You get served what you deserve. Harrison was a good man who ended up flying off the rails. If Whiskey had stayed in Rocky Cliff instead of coming here and telling everyone she was the last one to talk to him alive, she wouldn't have been struck by an icicle. Just saying..." Beck marched into his office only to return a few minutes later with a folder that he slapped on top of Whiskey's accident report.

"Tobin did some digging on Brook after she received the first note. You may want to read this before buying everything that exits her pretty mouth."

* * *

It always amazed Raven to see the difference forty-eight hours could make.

The fever was gone, and Eja had regained most of his energy and appetite, even though he still favoured ice cream over vegetables. "Ready, munchkin?"

Her son's big blue eyes sparkled with glee and an ingenuous smile embedded cute dimples on his rosy cheeks.

She kissed the top of his nose, then lowered his visor. Eja enjoyed snowmobile rides in the forest, and she loved spending time outdoors with him. By next winter, his legs should be long enough to snowshoe. She looked forward to those new memories waiting on the horizon. His small mitts gripped the back of her parka. If he needed something, he knew to tug three times.

Raven headed for the bridge.

In the last few days, the threats against her had haunted her every waking moment, even spilling into her dreams. This morning, she had driven to town to get some food. At the entrance of the grocery store, there was a huge bulletin board where residents pinned ads, selling anything from trucks to baby clothes. She had read all the handwritten cards. None had displayed capital *Ps* or *Bs* similar to the ones in the notes.

If I hadn't made copies before handing the notes over, I may never have noticed the perp's distinctive handwriting. Her mind travelled back to the first note she had received shortly after Gage's disappearance.

There was no telling how long he had been dead. Whoever tried to scare her away might not have wanted her to venture near the bridge and stumble prematurely onto his body. If this was the reason behind the notes, then someone had gone through a great deal of trouble to keep his death a secret. The far-fetched scenario invoked cover-up, and possibly murder.

Months of undercover investigation had taught her that nothing was impossible. Innocent lives could be bought, sold, or terminated in the blink of an eye. Gramp's declining health had given her a valid excuse to come home and a chance to rebuild her shattered life. Eja's birth had further grounded her, given her purpose, but the cost of raising him had chipped at her savings. She couldn't afford to move even if she wanted to. Her current position at Child Welfare Services in Sprucetown didn't pay as much as her previous one, despite carrying a heavier caseload. Still, she had investigated challenging cases in Sprucetown in the last five years—cases she wouldn't have come across in Halifax.

The possible connection between Gage's death and the threatening notes leaped at her. "How on earth did I miss it?" Except back in November, she hadn't known Gage was buried not too far from her cabin. Still, ignorance wasn't an excuse.

The bridge loomed closer, a series of logs tied together with leather straps that were stronger than the rusty nails securing the remaining handrail. An ominous landmark lost in the wilderness.

She stopped the snowmobile near the broken post and recalled the dreadful discovery. In her mind, the blurry image of Gage and his snowmobile slowly overlapped with the winter scenery.

Only the tip of a ski had protruded. The amount of snow it had taken to bury the snowmobile skis up and taillight down suggested Gage had crashed early in the winter, before Mother Nature unleashed her full wrath upon the forest.

The narrow window of opportunity for Gage to die in the stream flashed in front of her eyes. "The crash happened no later than mid-December."

Eja tapped her shoulder three times, then pointed at the forest.

The wind had intensified, and snow swirled in the air. Through the white mist, she glimpsed a shadow.

A blink later, it was gone.

                    * * *

Ever since Landon had been assigned to
the Sprucetown detachment, being buried
under paperwork had taken a more literal
sense. On the left corner of his desk were the
cases he had inherited from Harrison, and
on the right, the new cases that had landed
on his lap since his arrival.

Whiskey's death had been relegated to
the bottom of the right pile, buried
underneath two acts of vandalism, an
accusation of school bullying, a bar fight that
spilled into the street, spawning a dozen
disturbance calls and eight arrests for public
intoxication, and one count of family
violence. The belligerent husband was in
custody along with the eight obnoxious
goons sobering up in the drunk tank.

Curses and protests coming from the jail
cells wafted down the corridor, feeding the
headache burgeoning in Landon's temples.

Alone on the graveyard shift, he drank
another cup of coffee.

He was proud of his hacking skills, but
despite all his attempts, Harrison's deleted
messages and files remained out of reach.
The technician who erased his personal data
had either done a thorough job, or Harrison
had never filed the information on his work
computer.

Where is the bloody evidence you

unearthed, Harrison? When faced with a dead end, experience had taught Landon to take a step back and work on something else while his brain drilled a way out.

He flipped through Harrison's old cases. Names, violations... Nothing rang a bell or stood out.

Why do I have the feeling that I'm looking in all the wrong places? The thought brought his mind back to Raven's situation.

Tobin's handwritten report on her had raised more questions than answers, but it ruled him out as the author of the notes. The *Ps* and *Bs* didn't match. The same ended up being true for Beck.

If Tobin or Beck had been involved, it could have explained why they didn't take the threats against Raven seriously. Now they have no excuse other than indifference, negligence, or incompetence.

Disillusioned, Landon entered the archive room to retrieve her grandfather's murder report. The five-year-old report was dated February 10th.

*Marcel   Marshall.
Seventy-one years old. Cause
of death: fractured skull.*

A series of photos showed the elderly man lying in the snow, his head clobbered in a similar fashion to Raven's fox. An autopsy report detailed the numerous injuries Marshall sustained during the attack. It was signed by Dr. R. Gags.

When no inconsistency jumped out, Landon turned his attention to the police report in which Raven stated she had found her grandfather in the forest and glimpsed three suspects fleeing the scene. No worthy physical descriptions of the individuals had been recorded. A week later, Harrison had discovered the bodies of two indigenous teenagers near the crime scene. Fifteen-year-old Percy Foley and sixteen-year-old Nelson Bourke.

The bottom of the page sported the signature of Constable Gage Harrison.

Is that how you earned your promotion to corporal, Harrison? By solving the Marshall case?

Attached to the next page was the unsigned suicide note found in Bourke's pocket confessing to the murder.

Landon read the note, only to do a double-take at the capital *Ps* and *Bs*.

* * *

After a long nightshift spent pondering the implications of the suicide note, Landon released the jailbirds on their own recognizance and left the detachment.

In need of strong coffee, he drove across town to his favourite donut shop. In the midst of a quiet neighbourhood, he spotted

Beck's SUV parked alongside a deserted playground.

It's not seven-thirty yet, Beck, what are you doing here? His sergeant lived in a different neighbourhood, and Landon hadn't heard of any disturbance that could have drawn an officer here.

At the stop sign, Landon turned right on the street where the Harrisons lived.

A shadowy silhouette skirted Harrison's garage. From the street, it appeared to wear a uniform, but it vanished before Landon could get a better look.

Unsure if he should trust his sleep-deprived senses or draw a parallel between the silhouette and Beck's SUV, Landon parked in front of Harrison's residence.

A light shone in a window on the second floor.

Unless time was of the essence, Landon didn't visit or interview witnesses before eight in the morning or after nine at night, but the light led him to make an exception.

On his way to the front door, he gazed up and down the street. A lamppost flickered, but there was no sign of the silhouette. He rang the doorbell then rubbed his spiky chin, waiting.

The door swung open.

"What the hell do—" A visibly irate widow glared at him in sudden confusion. "Corporal Steele?"

"Mrs. Harrison." Landon stepped inside and closed the door behind him to stop the cold from invading the entryway. "Sorry for the early intrusion, but I saw a light in your window and—"

Over her shoulder, he peeked a shadow at the top of the stairs. Harrison's widow tensed turning around.

A child in a teal nightgown, a shade lighter than her mother's bathrobe, tiptoed down the stairs hugging a teddy bear against her chest. "Mama, I'm hungry. The man—"

"It's okay, baby." Harrison's widow rushed to the bottom of the stairs and scooped her daughter in her arms. "It's just Corporal Steele."

Landon tucked his cap under his arm, waiting.

The widow returned into the lobby with her daughter who had stuck a thumb in her mouth. "For the record, I keep the light in the upstairs bathroom on all night, but since we're all awake, thanks to you, will you tell me why you're here, and make it brief?"

The edge in her voice didn't escape Landon. *I should have taken a nap, got my coffee, and let her have hers, before questioning her.* "I'm closing your husband's cases, ma'am, but some files are incomplete. Do you know if he kept any documents at home? In a filing cabinet perhaps, or on his home computer?"

Harrison's daughter stared with dark brown eyes, sporting the same ambiguous expression as Raven's son. The two children appeared to be the same age.

"No, he didn't." Harrison's widow repositioned her daughter, tucking her head against the crook of her neck. "Gage didn't bring his work home, only his pathetic self. If that's all, I'd like to make breakfast for my daughter."

"I'm sorry to have bothered you, ma'am." While the woman's attitude toward her husband couldn't be clearer, or more understandable, Landon couldn't help but wish for a valid excuse to search her house. *The bloody evidence has to be somewhere.*

Chapter 5

Landon parked his RCMP truck near the entrance of Raven's long, snow-covered driveway, then walked toward her cabin.

Someone had built a snow fort on the front yard. A child in a blue snowsuit climbed the icy rampart followed by the three-legged German Shepherd.

Landon made eye contact with Raven's son. "Hi, little man. Where's your mom?"

Rusty barked once in response while Eja pointed at the shed without uttering a word.

Landon wasn't fond of noisy children, but the quiet boy reminded him of himself at the same age. "You're the strong silent type, aren't you?"

His face scrunched up in obvious puzzlement, Eja retreated into the corner of his snow fort where he cuddled with his dog.

Landon extended an arm. "Want to come with me to see your mom?"

The boy shook his head side to side.

Unsure how to interpret the silent treatment or the refusal, Landon headed toward the shed. Thumping sounds resonated from where the fox had hung. He rounded the corner.

Dressed in jeans and plaid shirt, Raven was chopping wood. Sweat trickled down her face and the shirt hugged her heaving chest.

"Raven!"

The lack of response stopped him dead in his tracks. On the spur of the moment, he had forgotten she couldn't hear.

How am I supposed to get the attention of a woman holding an axe without startling her and jeopardizing both our lives? No wonder Eja didn't show any inclination to accompany me. For his own safety, the child had probably been taught to stay away from his mother until she fetched him.

Without getting too close, Landon waved his arms while trying to move into her line of vision. Focused on her task, she paid no attention to him. Resigned to wait until she finished, he backtracked.

A snowball flew by him and hit the bundle of logs. Raven's head snapped up, and she looked above her shoulder.

Landon followed her gaze to the boy slapping his mitts together. "Thank you, little man."

Eja sauntered away, the dog on his heels.

"Landon?" With one hand, Raven embedded the axe into a large tree stump, then headed toward the shed. "What are you doing here?"

"I could ask you the same question." He followed her to a pile of wood stacked neatly against the outside wall.

Her parka lay on the top of the cord. She put it on but didn't zip it. "Chopping wood. Wasn't that obvious?"

"Need help?" Many questions swirled in his mind, questions he ached to ask, but he reined in his impatience. First and foremost, he needed to gain her trust. Only then could he hope for truthful answers. "If you let me take a few practice swings, I'm pretty sure I can manage to split a few logs."

"Practice swings? You do realize that doesn't sound too safe, right?" Mischievousness trickled through her smile, a smile as vibrant as the untamed wilderness surrounding them. "If you help me carry the wood inside, I'll make you a mug of hot chocolate for your trouble."

* * *

Raven gestured toward the kitchen. "Why don't we sit at the table?"

Her son had fallen asleep on the couch watching Landon stack wood in a corner, and she didn't want to disturb his peaceful rest.

"I haven't had hot chocolate in ages." The officer licked his upper lip after taking a sip from his mug. "Thank you."

The soft glow in his dark brown eyes warmed her insides. Too many years had passed since she welcomed a man into her cabin and let him take off his boots. While he worked, Landon had also removed his gun and stored it on top of the fridge, beyond Eja's reach, to avoid an accident. An officer trusting her with his weapon had brought back bittersweet memories, and she found herself wishing she could lower not only her guard but also the drawbridge keeping her heart safe.

Her visitor cupped his mug with both hands. "Will Eja ask for hot chocolate when he wakes up?"

"He doesn't ask for anything anymore." When Landon arched a brow, Raven realized she had thought aloud, a bad habit she had developed in her teens. "I didn't mean—"

"Has something happened to Eja?" Landon gazed at her with a strange mixture of compassion and curiosity.

"Something happened last November, but I don't know what. It'd snowed the previous days, so Eja took his little red shovel into his treehouse to play while I chopped wood. Rusty was with him..." The ill-fated day replayed in her mind as clearly as if it had happened this morning.

She had raised her axe above her head, ready to swing, when—without warning—Eja had appeared in front of her. A few seconds later and she might have hurt him, but the axe had slipped from her hands and grazed her back before landing in the snow somewhere behind her.

"Eja knows to stay away from me when I hold any type of weapon. If he needs me, he throws something in front of me to catch my attention. That day, he didn't warn me. He just walked up to me, shivering like a leaf in a storm. His face was whiter than snow and his bare hands colder than ice. He was... he was petrified. Rusty was by his side, her tail between her legs. I picked him up and marched to the house. Rusty limped on my heels. There were blood and snowmobile tracks in the fresh snow near his treehouse. I thought someone had come and hurt my son. I called Caleb. He rushed here." Though her brother wasn't a vet, he had examined both Eja and Rusty. "Caleb didn't find any physical signs of assault, but Eja hasn't spoken or played near the treehouse since that day."

Landon nodded slowly. "Did you mention the incident with Eja when you reported the first threatening note?"

"No, I—" Her son lost his voice on November 15th. She didn't receive the first note until December 1st. "Two weeks had already elapsed. It never occurred to me there might be a connection between the two incidents." Angry and frustrated, she stared at the contents of her mug. *How could I have been so blind?*

"Raven, I need to ask you about your grandfather Marshall." He glanced over his shoulder toward the couch and then leaned forward. "What happened the day he was murdered? It's very important."

"Why?" That day was etched into her memory as a turning point in her life. "That was five years ago."

"I know, but you have to trust me. Please?"

She didn't know if she could still trust, but the consideration he showed toward small details made her inclined to give him a chance. "You know he wasn't my real grandfather, right?"

"From what I heard, he raised you, and he raised you well." A peaceful glow shone in his eyes, softening his roguish face. "In my book, that makes him your grandfather."

The compliment and veracity of his words heartened her. "Gramp was recovering from an infection. The doctor had ordered him to rest, not that Gramp knew the meaning of rest. That February morning, he wanted to check the two traps he'd set where the river splits in two. He usually rode his snowmobile, but it was such a beautiful and warm winter day, he decided to snowshoe. He gave me a kiss and left around nine." She had offered to go with him, but he had turned her down with the promise of being back by lunchtime. "He was an outdoor man who enjoyed the solitude of the forest. The return trek is about three hours. When he missed lunch, I... I felt something was wrong. I hopped on my snowmobile and searched for him. I found him by the boulder near the river, beaten to death. His snowshoes were missing. He'd made them himself and attached a rabbit paw to each one. For luck."

"I'm sorry." Landon's face reflected his sincerity. "I read your grandfather's report. At the time, you implicated three people. Would you elaborate, please?"

She hadn't believed the two teenagers to be responsible. Their homes were searched, but Gramp's snowshoes were never recovered. Gage had investigated her claims and come up empty-handed.

"When I arrived, I saw three people disappearing into the forest on the other side of the river. Two looked like grown-up men, but the third could have been a teenager. They had to wear snowshoes or else they would have sunk in the snow. Did I see their faces? No, I only saw them from behind. Did I see any of them kill my grandfather? No, Gramp was already dead. Do I believe they were somehow implicated? Yes, or else they wouldn't have left Gramp's body there. Do I expect you to believe me?" Raven shrugged off the rhetorical question. "I was so distressed over Gramp's killing, it never occurred to me to chase after them, but now I wish I had."

"If you'd caught up with them, they would have killed you, too. It's a good thing you didn't." A lopsided smile softened his expression. "I'd like to show you something, but it needs to stay between us."

Stunned that he might believe her,

Raven could only acquiesce.

"I made copies of the notes you received, and the suicide note found with the teenagers accused of killing your grandfather." Landon pulled out folded papers from his pocket and then unfolded them on the table in front of her. "Look at them and tell me if anything strikes you as odd."

Though she remembered Gage telling her about the confession, she had never laid eyes on the note itself.

> *Old man Marshall caught us drinking and sniffing glue. He wouldn't leave us alone. Percy didn't mean to bash his head. We don't want to go to prison. Booze and drugs ruined our lives. We want to die.*

Reading the confession after all these years didn't bring any closure. As her gaze lingered on the reasons behind Gramp's murder, the curly *P* in *Percy* and the *B* in *Booze* jumped at her.

"It's the same handwriting, but it can't be." Her eyes were betraying her. "The teenagers are dead, Landon. They can't be the ones who wrote the threatening notes dropped on my porch, not unless—"

The only possible explanation punched her in the guts, uprooting her past.

Unable to sleep, Landon stared at the ceiling of his bedroom. In the dark, he couldn't see the fan rotating clockwise, but when he closed his eyes, he saw Raven's shocked expression.

He could pinpoint the exact moment that realization had struck her. The speed at which she connected the dots and reached the same conclusion he did had made him proud. Unfortunately, she hadn't been able to shed any new light on her grandfather's death. Still, Landon was convinced she had glimpsed the real killers.

"It means the two suicides aren't suicides. I'm now dealing with three unsolved murders and possibly three killers on the prowl for Raven. But why five years later?"

No matter from which angle Landon looked at it, he couldn't fathom a plausible motive behind the killers' puzzling behaviours.

"One of the killers wrote the suicide note. Then last December, he or they started threatening Raven. What happened to change the status quo?"

The first thing that came to his mind was Harrison's disappearance and murder.

"Harrison investigated Marshall's

murder and the suicides. This can't be a coincidence."

Landon needed the mysterious evidence that Harrison had unearthed. "What did you do with it? Gave it to Whiskey along with your badge?"

The idea that the stripper might have lied about just talking resurfaced every time Landon sat in his truck.

All the vehicles in the fleet were cleaned and washed regularly. The odds that any DNA evidence from three months ago was still present in his truck were lower than zero.

"Bloody hell, Steele. Forget it. You're not going to find anything." Agreeing with himself didn't stop him from getting out of bed.

* * *

The light beams cut through the darkness, illuminating the snowy road leading to town. By the time Raven reached Caleb's house, she had encountered three coyotes and two moose, a mother with her calf, the offspring grazing her bumper. Had she applied the brakes a fraction of a second later, her old station wagon would have ended up at the scrapyard, the calf in a freezer, and herself in one of Caleb's refrigerated bays.

She was seeking her brother, but not in that manner.

Caleb's green Hummer wasn't parked in his driveway, and he never kept it in his garage. It didn't fit alongside the minivan he bought his girlfriend Annette for Christmas. Her brother was ready to start a family, but Annette seemed oblivious to his desire. The big house he built on an acre of land outside Sprucetown was another clue that Annette had yet to decipher.

Seeing no sign of the Hummer in his sleepy neighbourhood, Raven drove to his medical clinic. His green monster was parked near the side door, a door he never locked when he was on the premises.

With Eja in her arms, she walked down the well-lit staircase and found her brother in the morgue, working on paperwork.

"How can you trade a warm bed for a freezing basement?" she teased, though in his place, she would trade Annette's body for a stuffed owl.

"If it isn't my favourite sister." He greeted her with a hug before taking Eja from her arms. "And my favourite nephew. How are you doing, buddy?"

Half asleep in his snowsuit, her son leaned his head against his uncle's shoulder. "Eja's doing better. That's not why I'm here."

"It's not?" Caleb gave her a dubious look. "It's five in the morning. You should be in bed."

She had turned and tossed all night

thinking about the suicide note. "Landon came to visit me yesterday."

"You mean Officer Steele?" A smile crept on Caleb's face. "Are you seeing him?"

"No, I'm not." She didn't even want to know how that idea entered her brother's skull. "He's..." If she told him everything Landon shared, Caleb would worry and insist she come to live in his new house. She wasn't ready to move, she might never be. Besides, involving him might place his life in jeopardy. It wasn't a risk she was willing to take when there was nothing he could do to change the situation she found herself in.

After a sleepless night, focusing on Caleb's lips already required all the mental effort Raven could muster. She didn't care if her twisted reasoning wasn't logical as long as it rang true.

"He seems like a nice guy, Raven. If he's interested, you shouldn't reject him offhandedly. A boy needs a father."

Her brother had never pried into her private life, and of all the mornings to breach the subject of Eja's paternity, this wasn't a good one. "I'm not here to discuss Eja, okay?"

Caleb raised a hand in surrender. "What can I do for you?"

"I need a huge favour." Her brother had never refused her anything, but she had also never abused the privilege. "I need to look at the autopsy reports of Gramp and the two teenagers accused of killing him."

Alone in the RCMP garage, Landon checked the only place that could have been overlooked during cleaning. Under the seats.

He illuminated every inch with his flashlight. No stains, not even a crumb of the blueberry muffin he had eaten the other morning.

Nothing. Whoever was hired to clean the vehicles was even more meticulous than his grandmother. *I should have stayed in bed.*

As he rolled sideways to extricate himself, he twisted his neck, and out of the corner of his eye, he caught something yellow. Puzzled, he shined the light upward.

Bloody luck. A large yellow envelope was taped underneath the seat. Landon pulled it out. *That better be it, Harrison.*

Built halfway between the detachment and his mobile home, the garage was visible from both places. Aside from his truck, three other RCMP vehicles and half a dozen snowmobiles were parked inside. Every officer had access to the garage. Landon couldn't take the chance that anyone saw him walking home with a big yellow envelope.

Before getting out of his truck, he slipped the envelope inside his jacket and zipped it.

A draft of cold air swept inside the garage.

"Steele? What are you doing here this early?"

I could ask you the same question, Tobin. Landon slammed the door of his truck. Feigning irritation and lying came easily when addressing the constable. "I can't find my fob. I thought maybe I'd dropped it under the seat, but no such luck. I guess I'll go home and search my closet again."

* * *

Raven understood about privacy rules and regulations, but Gramp was family, and one could argue the two teenagers fell under the jurisdiction of Child Welfare Services.

In the rearview mirror, she caught Eja's reflection. Wide-awake, he was playing with a toy car, transforming it into a robot. It was a gift from Caleb after he refused her request.

You're not forgiven yet, Big Brother. Vexed by his refusal, she stopped at the arena. She had driven into town for answers, and she refused to return home empty-handed. "Come on, munchkin. We'll go inside for a few minutes."

The curling rink was deserted, the snack bar was closed, but the hockey rink was open. Kids in blue or green jerseys chased a black puck on the ice under the frantic gestures of their coaches.

Eja climbed into the bleachers to watch the game while she browsed through the numerous ads pinned to the bulletin board.

No *Bs* or *Ps*. "Five years ago, I missed something. I need to go back to the river where Gramp died. This afternoon I'll—"

Sensing a presence, she spun around. A guy with dark brown eyes and a buzz cut stared intently at her from the doorway of the men's dressing room.

A hockey bag was slung over his shoulder, and his mouth formed an O. He quickly diverted his gaze and strode away.

* * *

Seated at his kitchen table with the doors locked and blinds closed, Landon sipped on a bad cup of coffee while silently reading the first report he had pulled out of the yellow envelope. *November 10th, five drunken men were arrested for disorderly conduct—*

This report was an exact copy of the one Landon had found on his desk when he first reported to Sprucetown. It had taken him more time to set a password on his computer than to close and file that case.

I obviously missed something, or else Harrison wouldn't have bothered hiding it

83

in his truck.

The five men in question were arrested at The Polar Skin for exchanging insults and blows. In the shuffle, a few tables were damaged. They sobered up in the drunk tank and were sent home the next morning.

According to this report, four of them had no prior record, but the last man, Noel Foley, was flagged with a star. Shoplifting was written beside his name.

"Now that's odd," Landon muttered under his breath. The report on his desk had made no mention of shoplifting.

Landon flipped to the next page and frowned. The handwriting was different. It took him a few seconds to realize he was looking at Foley's shoplifting arrest.

As Landon read over the report, he summarized the information in his mind. *Five years ago, twenty-four-year-old Noel Foley and his fifteen-year-old cousin were arrested for shoplifting and received probation and community service. The younger cousin was referred to the juvenile court.*

"Talk to me, Harrison. What does Noel Foley have—" Speaking the name aloud highlighted a possible connection. "Is he Percy Foley's cousin by any chance?"

Chapter 6

Landon entered the detachment. "Tobin? Sarge? Anyone in?"

The door of Beck's office was open, but the sergeant wasn't on the premises. Tobin's desk was unoccupied. The jail cells at the end of the corridor were empty and clean.

Their absence gave Landon the opportunity to snoop into the old reports stored in Beck's office and the archive room.

An hour later, he slammed the last drawer shut. There was no record of Noel Foley ever having been arrested prior to the drunken mishap, but the copy of the shoplifting arrest made by Harrison indicated otherwise.

A door banged and footsteps resonated inside the building.

Landon hurried out of the archive room and met with Beck in the corridor. "Morning, Sarge."

"I heard from Alessi Harrison." His sergeant glared at him. "She wasn't happy to be harassed at seven in the morning."

Not the least intimidated, Landon leaned one shoulder against the wall. "I thought Harrison might have kept some work files at home." The encounter had happened days ago. "For the record, it was closer to seven-thirty, and I didn't harass her."

"Don't be a smartass. I convinced Alessi not to lodge a formal complaint. In your place, I'd count my lucky stars and stay the heck away from her." Beck poked a finger at Landon's tie, intruding upon his personal space. "Got it?"

Landon didn't recall acting inappropriately, but his sergeant had obviously bought whatever exited the widow's pretty mouth. *That's bias, Beck.* "Alessi Harrison is out of bounds. Got it, Sergeant."

* * *

From his desk, Landon kept one eye on Beck's closed door and the other on his computer screen while searching the database for Foley's shoplifting arrest report.

Where are you, Foley? Once he exhausted all authorized and unauthorized avenues, Landon hacked into the backup system and searched the deleted files.

The sergeant's office door opened. Landon rushed to erase his tracks, but not before glimpsing what he had been looking for.

"A truck rear-ended a car in the Tim Hortons's parking lot." Standing in the doorway with his jacket in his hands, Beck looked at the window. "The vehicles block the drive-thru and the customers aren't happy. I should be back in a few hours."

For a moment, Landon feared he would be sent out to take care of disgruntled patrons too lazy to park their trucks and walk ten feet to get inside the donut shop.

When Beck exited, Landon heaved a silent sigh of relief.

A copy of Foley's arrest still existed, buried deep within the deleted files. Someone had gone through lots of trouble to make Foley disappear—someone with access to the database—but that someone had forgotten the backup system.

Harrison hadn't trusted his colleagues, and he had taken precautions, but he still ended up dead.

The front door opened. Tobin stepped in.

"Tobin." Landon leaned back in his chair. "How long have you been stuck here?"

"Two years." His colleague frowned. "Why?"

Because I'm suspecting an inside job. "What about Beck? How long has he been here?"

"Three years." Tobin tossed his winter jacket on his chair. "And in case you haven't noticed, he's counting the weeks till retirement. If I were you, I wouldn't screw it for him."

Duly noted. And ignored. "I'm going for a snowmobile ride. I'll be back later."

* * *

The pill that Raven fed her son was bigger than the peas in his plate. The ease with which Eja swallowed it attested to his recovery. Meanwhile, mealtime wouldn't be as frustrating if only he gave the same swift treatment to his green vegetables.

"Munchkin, please hurry to empty your plate, or else we may not have time to go on a long snowmobile ride."

Eja speared a pea with his fork, gave it a dubious look, then dropped it on the floor. Rusty sniffed the pea. Her ears drooped down, she retreated under the table, leaving the vegetable where it landed.

"Rusty..." Raven heaved a sigh. "You don't have to agree with Eja."

A mischievous grin split her son's face, only to fade seconds later. Rusty hurried out of the room as Eja knocked into thin air.

"You stay here and finish your plate. Understood?" Raven went to answer the door. Surprised to see Landon, she stared at his face. "Are you all right?"

The dark stubble spiking on his chin and the even darker circles under his eyes accentuated his fatigue. "I'm not getting enough sleep. May I come in?"

"Sure." She hadn't even closed the door, and Rusty had already brought Landon her toy. "She likes you, but feel free to ignore her."

Landon removed his gloves, squatted down, and then stroked Rusty's head. "Hello, girl." The dog nuzzled against his neck, like she did with Eja. "I haven't had a female warming up to my charming personality in ages. If you don't mind, I'll take all the affection I can get."

Astonishment sizzled inside Raven's chest. With his forthright personality, he was the last officer she would have pictured unattached. "You're an interesting character. Why don't you sit down?"

"We need to talk." He tossed Rusty's toy across the room. "In private."

"Eja is practising his magic trick in the kitchen." The look that Raven ventured over her shoulder confirmed her son hadn't moved. "He may be there for a while."

Landon took off his boots and unzipped his jacket. "What magic trick?"

"He's trying to make his veggies disappear without eating them." Her dog dashed into the kitchen with her toy, leaving them alone. "Unfortunately for him, Rusty has an aversion to peas."

At her invitation, Landon followed her to the couch, where he sat beside her.

He leaned toward her, and his knee

brushed her leg. "Do you recall if Sergeant Beck or Constable Tobin were brought in five years ago to investigate your grandfather's death?"

His proximity made it harder to concentrate on what he said.

"No... not to my knowledge. Gage led the investigation. Sergeant..." She couldn't recall his name, but he had been too busy romancing a town councillor's wife to interfere with Gage's investigation. "Whoever was the sergeant at the time didn't get involved. Why?"

"Does the name Noel Foley ring a bell?" He tactically deflected her question with one of his own. "Harrison arrested him last November for disturbance, but Foley was also arrested five years ago for shoplifting. He would have been twenty-four at that time."

"F-O-L-E-Y?" To dispel any confusion, she had spelled his last name. "I don't recall a Noel Foley, but wasn't one of the teenagers accused of Gramp's murder named Foley?"

Landon nodded. "A few months before your grandfather's death, Noel Foley and his fifteen-year-old cousin lifted over-the-counter medication from a drugstore. I believe Percy to be Noel's cousin. Since you're a social worker and the younger cousin was referred to Child Welfare Services, I was hoping you might have heard of one or both."

A connection had to exist between both

Foleys and the events surrounding her grandfather's death, or else Landon wouldn't be asking these questions.

"If Percy is in the system, I should have access to his file." Her Internet connection was slow at times, but it rarely stopped her from using her laptop. "Is that an official request?"

Wrinkles formed at the corner of Landon's mouth. "I'd rather no one knew about the request."

"I see..." Not having to drag Eja along while she revisited the site where Gramp died would allow her more freedom of movement and save her time. "I need to go for a snowmobile ride. In exchange for an unofficial look at the files, would you babysit my son?"

* * *

Landon didn't know how many peas had originally filled Eja's plate, but all the remaining ones showed signs of stabbing. "You really don't like peas, do you?"

The youngster vehemently shook his head.

"You're lucky I'm hungry." In two forkfuls, Landon emptied the plate. "Don't tell your mom, or she'll ground me."

When he picked up the stunned boy and lowered him to the floor, a shy smile blossomed on Eja's face. As much as Landon disliked disputing Raven's authority, missing a snowmobile ride was punishment enough.

"Go brush your teeth. Then you and Rusty can play in front of the fireplace while I work on your mom's computer."

Before leaving the cabin, Raven had logged into her account to check her work schedule and *inadvertently* forgotten to log out.

Landon typed Percy Foley into the search engine. "Let's see what we have in plain sight."

Something hit his foot, and gleeful laughter echoed in the room. His attention divided between the screen and the loud duo playing on the floor, Landon tossed the squeaky rubber toy across the living room. The three-legged German Shepherd grabbed it first, only to be pounced on by her human companion.

A new page scrolled down the computer screen.

Percy Foley. Fifteen years old.

Finding out the teenager was in the system heartened Landon.

Arrested for shoplifting with his cousin Noel Foley.

More information appeared on the screen. Landon would have kissed the owner of the laptop if she had sat beside him.

The venue struck Landon as unusual and interesting.

Landon would like a clerk to man the front counter at the detachment, a meticulous clerk like the one who wrote this report.

"Hold on a sec." According to the police report, Gramp Marshall was killed around lunchtime on February 10th. "Percy had a solid alibi for that day. This proves someone framed him for Marshall's murder."

Eja bounced on the cushion next to Landon and stared at him with his mother's

93

eyes.

The boy deserved a reward for behaving properly in his mother's absence, and Landon needed some fresh air to clear his mind. "Go get dressed and don't forget your helmet. I'm taking you and your dog for a snowmobile ride around the cabin while we wait for your mom."

* * *

A giant boulder, its top covered with an uneven snowy wig and its rough-rounded greyish body peppered with flurries, added character to the peaceful clearing where the river split in two. If not for the total lack of vegetation peeking through the snow, someone unfamiliar with these parts of the forest might mistake the ice underneath for solid ground.

Raven parked her snowmobile at the edge of the trees and left her helmet on the seat. Multiple snowmobile tracks crisscrossed the clearing and the frozen river. She walked in a track toward the boulder where her grandfather died. Movement on her right caught her eye. She shifted her gaze and froze.

A bulky man in a black snowsuit looked in her direction.

Shivers coursed through her body. She couldn't see his eyes through the slits of his ski mask, but the walking stick he brandished and his menacing stance added an ominous element to his puzzling presence in the clearing.

Raven glanced over her shoulder, taking a step back.

A slender man wearing similar gear blocked the path to her snowmobile. He followed the prints she had made, quickly closing the gap between them.

"What do you want?" The words came out of her mouth in ragged breaths.

She didn't see his mouth move through the hole of his ski mask, but whether or not he answered her became irrelevant the moment that she realized the question didn't slow his advance.

That can't bold well... An invisible hand squeezed her insides, unleashing her survival instincts. She charged at the slender man, catching him off balance. Her bodycheck sent him tumbling in the snow.

She rushed past him, hopped on her snowmobile, and plowed ahead. The bulky man dashed to block her path and raised his stick. She swerved to avoid him.

The stick connected with her head.

* * *

All bundled up, his helmet strapped over his head, Eja trudged in the snow alongside

Rusty, reminding Landon of his long walks with his father and a little rat terrier named Coral.

As a teenager, Landon had become stranded in the cold for hours after his snowmobile stalled and refused to start again. If not for his father rescuing him before nightfall, Landon might have met an early death. The incident taught him caution and preparedness. From then on, he had taken the habit of towing a cargo sled in which he kept extra fuel and survival gear, including his police issue snowshoes. "Do you think Rusty will like riding in the sled behind my snowmobile?"

The boy nodded, but then he kept his head tilted back and stopped.

Landon followed Eja's gaze to a small log cabin built in a huge deciduous tree, complete with an angled roof and holes in place of windows. Foot-long boards were hammered onto the trunk at regular intervals, leading up to a square opening in the middle of the floor.

"I had a treehouse too when I was a little boy." Landon crouched down, putting himself at eye level with the youngster. "Would you show me what yours looks like inside?"

The boy glanced back and forth between Landon and the tree, his expression reflecting his fear.

"I'll tell you a secret. When I chase bad guys, I try to be brave, but deep down here..."

Landon poked at his own chest. "I'm always scared."

Eja's eyes grew wider.

"It's hard to be brave, it's very hard, but we have to try, right?" As much as it pained Landon to ask the boy to relive his nightmare, finding out what terrified him would go a long way toward helping him cope and hopefully heal. "I'll tell you another secret. If you and I climb up together, we'll be *twice* as brave, and that will make you a very courageous little man. So, you think we can have a peek inside your treehouse?"

Eja moved his head into something resembling a reluctant nod, then hugged his dog.

"I think Rusty should come too. How about she goes first?" When the boy didn't object, Landon pushed the fifty-plus-pound dog up the makeshift ladder rung. "Good job, Rusty," he praised, impressed by the three-legged dog's agility. "Your turn, little man."

Landon followed the boy through the floor opening and crawled inside the treehouse.

At its highest point, the slanted ceiling reached almost five feet. Though high enough for a child to stand up, Eja didn't, nor did he approach any of the two windows. Instead, he retreated into the corner of the two solid walls with Rusty.

What secret is locked in your head, little man? Down on his hands and knees, Landon searched for clues. One window looked out onto Raven's house and shed. He inched closer to the other window. Multiple snowmobile tracks led in and out of the forest, but no signs of Raven yet. *Did you see someone in the forest?*

At a loss to make sense of the events that traumatized the boy, Landon absent-mindedly brushed off the snow on the ledge of the window, uncovering something yellow wedged in the corner of the frame.

This can't be... Landon picked up the yellow mitt and flipped it over. On its back was a black star, an identical match to the mitt found in Harrison's pocket.

Rattled by the discovery, he looked at Eja.

The boy had recoiled further into the corner, his dog curled into a ball next to him. Tears glistened in his eyes.

Eja walked up to me, his bare hands colder than ice. These had been Raven's words when she described the traumatizing afternoon.

Caleb got it wrong. The mitt never belonged to Harrison's daughter. Landon approached the frightened boy and sat beside him. "This is your mitt, isn't it?"

The boy didn't answer, but he squeezed his dog's neck.

Where's the key to your mind, little man? None of the interview techniques that Landon had perfected over the years applied to a child. He felt like a rookie facing his first suspect. *If only the dog could talk...* A crazy idea popped into his mind. "If I ask Rusty a question, do you think she'll answer me?"

Eja's round face scrunched up into a quizzical frown.

"Let's try, okay?" By using Rusty as an intermediary, Landon hoped to bypass the boy's fears. "Rusty, does Eja like peas? If she says yes, you pet her head. If she says no, you rub her back."

The boy rubbed the reddish streaks in Rusty's fur.

"She's a smart dog." Heartened by the small victory, Landon swept the yellow mitt in front of the canine's eyes. "Rusty, is this Eja's mitt?"

In the cold winter air, Eja's ragged breath rose in misty bursts. For many long seconds, he remained motionless. Then he briefly touched his dog between the ears.

Pride swelled inside Landon's chest. *Good little man.* The only way the mitt could have ended up in Harrison's pocket was if he came to visit the day Eja lost his voice.

Raven hadn't mentioned any visitors, but she had noticed fresh snowmobile tracks near the treehouse. And blood.

Maybe she didn't see Harrison. Maybe Harrison spotted Eja up in the treehouse and stopped to talk to the boy, but never made it to the cabin.

In Landon's presence, Raven referred to his colleagues by their ranks or last names, but she called Harrison by his first name. It denoted a certain familiarity. "Rusty, the day

Eja lost his mitt, did Corporal Gage Harrison come to the treehouse to say hello?"

An engine roared in the distance. *Go for another ride, Raven. I need more time with your son.*

The dog wore a pink collar with a silver tag. It chimed when Eja rubbed her nose.

A myriad of emotions were reflected on the boy's face, and while Landon was at a loss to isolate one, he believed in the affirmative gesture.

Eja had seen Harrison from the window, and he might have lost his mitts waving. One landed on the ledge while the other came into Harrison's possession, possibly after landing in the snow below.

Why did Harrison put it in his pocket instead of climbing up the trunk and returning it right away? A possible reason came to Landon's mind. *Something stopped him.*

Someone slammed a door.

Raven was back. In a few minutes, she would climb up demanding to know what he was doing alone in the treehouse with Eja.

Landon was running out of time to obtain the answers he needed. "Eja, did you see someone else with Gage Harrison? A man, perhaps?"

The boy cupped his dog's head with both hands.

A child doesn't stop talking just because he witnesses an encounter between two men. Something else had frightened Eja. A possible answer flashed in red in front of Landon's eyes. *The blood in the snow.*

Raven slammed the door again. Once she saw the raw pain on her son's face, she was bound to shoot Landon with his own gun.

According to Caleb, the injuries sustained by Harrison could also have been the result of a vicious beating, not just a crash.

At this moment, Landon could think of only one scenario that explained both the blood and the boy's trauma. The encounter between Harrison and the other man had turned violent, so violent it left blood in the snow.

"Eja, the man you saw, did he hurt Gage Harrison?" Tears streaked down Eja's rosy cheeks, breaking Landon's heart. "Do you remember what that man looks like?"

Eja shook his head. The visor of his helmet slid down, obscuring his face.

"You were hiding with Rusty in the treehouse, weren't you?" He scooped the boy into his arms and hugged him. "You didn't do anything wrong, little man."

An engine roared to life, startling him.

Your son needs you, Raven. What are you up to? Landon stretched his neck toward the window and glimpsed a snowmobile whizzing away.

Stunned to see the rider wore a black jacket, and not a red parka, Landon rose to his knees. "Raven?"

An explosion resonated in his ears, throwing him and the boy in his arms to the floor.

* * *

Landon shielded the boy from the blast, but the pounding inside his skull was compounded by the weight of the roof on his back and the dog's whimpering. "It's okay, Rusty. Eja's fine."

The youngster gripped the front of his RCMP jacket. With Eja safe against his chest, Landon crawled on his knees toward the hole at the centre of the treehouse. The floor had withstood the shockwave. Nonetheless, he didn't want to test its solidity any longer than necessary. His slow progress toward the exit was marked by the sliding of timbers off his back. Through a gap, he glimpsed the ruins of Raven's cabin.

The devastation in his heart sank into the pit of his stomach. While no one could have survived that explosion, nothing indicated Raven had returned with the unknown rider and entered her cabin. Still, the untimely visit roused Landon's suspicion.

That explosion resonates like a deadly threat, not an accident. Landon cursed himself for not looking at the snowmobile when he first heard the engine. A fraction of a second was all it would have taken him to ascertain whether or not Raven had hitched a ride back. Until forensic evidence proved otherwise, Landon assumed she was still in the forest.

I'll take care of your son, Raven. Just stay safe, would you?

The dog shuddered, looking down the hole in the floor.

"Get down, Rusty." Landon nudged the animal down, eager to follow her.

Rusty jumped in the snow and scampered away.

The wood above Landon's head cracked.

Fearing an imminent collapse, he skipped the last few rungs, landing in the snow with Eja, and then hurried to clear the vicinity of the treehouse. "Rusty?" To Landon's dismay, the dog ran toward the forest. "Come back here, girl! Now!"

A deafening crash echoed in his ears. He didn't need to glance over his shoulder to know the treehouse had met the same fate as Raven's cabin.

"Close your eyes, little man." The safety of the only witness to Harrison's beating was Landon's priority, but he couldn't walk away from the crime scene without ascertaining Raven wasn't lying somewhere in the clearing, injured but alive.

His hand over Eja's visor to block his view, Landon searched the debris. The child shivered in his arms. Landon held the terrified boy tighter. "It'll be okay, little man."

The explosion had obliterated the cabin and damaged the shed but hadn't ignited any fire.

No matter where Landon looked, he saw no sign of human remains. *That's a good sign.*

An engine purred in the distance, ending Landon's search. His first thought was for Raven, but he was also aware that sometimes perpetrators returned to the scene of their crime.

I can't risk a confrontation with the wrong person. Not with Eja.

"We have to hide, little man, but I'll come back later to fetch Rusty. I promise."

Landon grabbed a branch full of needles, and as he hurried toward his snowmobile, he dragged it behind to fill his footprints with snow. Once he reached it, he lowered Eja on the seat.

"You sit in front and don't move." Landon started the engine. Its sound blended with the one coming from the approaching snowmobile. With any luck, the rider wouldn't pick up the sound of Landon's engine over his own. "We'll wait a few minutes in case it's your mom returning."

Landon retrieved a pair of binoculars from his saddlebag, then, standing upright on the seat, he pushed a branch aside and scanned the forest. Further past the shed, a light flickered between the trees. Landon zoomed in on the headlight.

The rider of the snowmobile wore a black jacket.

Time to go for a long ride and cover my tracks. No one could know that Landon witnessed the explosion, glimpsed a suspect, or took Eja into protective custody.

Chapter 7

The sun caressed the treetops, creating monstrous shadows on the fresh path that Landon beat along a frozen river.

In the forest, the temperature dropped sharply with the last rays of light. Wandering in the middle of nowhere after nightfall was reckless. He needed to take Eja somewhere safe, but he didn't trust anyone to care for him, not even the doctor.

Sorry, Caleb, but you have a lousy poker face. That's a strike against you.

Officially requesting protective custody when he distrusted everyone within the detachment equaled playing Russian roulette with Eja's life. Of all the scumbags that Landon had encountered in his career, corrupt officers were the ones he despised the most. Duty wasn't just a word, it was an oath—an oath he might be forced to break to protect an innocent boy.

On nights like this one, Landon longed for the carefree evenings he spent huddled around a campfire listening to his grandfather's stories.

A safe place popped in his mind. *The cottage.*

* * *

The soothing scent of burning wood teased her nostrils and the heat warmed her face. Wrapped in the sweet sensations, she stared at his image.

A boy... a cute little boy...

The image slipped out of reach. She made a fist in a futile attempt to recapture his image. Downy fur tangled between her fingers, awakening her senses. She opened her eyes. Flames undulated on a ceiling, highlighting strange protuberances. Unfamiliar with the sight, she moved her head, stirring a dull pain inside her skull.

Careful about making any sudden movements, she took in her surroundings. A fire burned in the middle of the cave. A cozy cave.

She lay on a soft, short-haired pelt, moose from the feel of it, with a black bear skin covering her up.

Sparks flew quietly and the flames climbed in the air, illuminating a water barrel. Mesmerized by the eerie silence, she stared at the woman poking a stick into the fire, its tip glowing like a neon red dot.

The woman turned in her direction and approached her bed. Her lips moved without making a sound, but amid the shadows created by the fire, some words registered. *Blow. Awake.*

"I... I can't hear you."

The elderly indigenous woman kneeled by her side. "I'm Meg." A kind smile softened her shrivelled face marred by a cruel scar. "What's your name, child?"

Unnerved by her ability to understand, she searched her memory for an explanation, only encountering an insurmountable void. "I... I can't remember."

* * *

Desperate times, desperate measures. Had Landon not been in a rush to leave Sprucetown, he would have bought a car seat instead of buckling the youngster directly on the back seat of his Jeep.

He drove to Port aux Basques, only stopping twice during the four-hour trip. Once on a deserted road to answer the nature calls of a wiggling boy, during which Landon also traded his uniform for the emergency civilian clothes he kept in his trunk. The second time was at a hospital in Corner Brook to make a collect call from a pay phone.

The ferry for Nova Scotia was scheduled to depart at 11:45 p.m. It gave him an hour and twenty minutes to orchestrate a coverup.

As he approached a gas station, he instructed Eja to lie on the seat, out of view. "You stay quiet, little man. I'll be right back."

While filling up on gas, Landon looked through the tinted window. Nothing moved inside the Jeep. Pride swelled inside his chest. *You're an awesome listener. Your mother would be proud.*

Landon entered the gas station and picked up a six-pack of beer and a can of tomato juice.

At the cash register, a teenage attendant played with his cell phone. He didn't lift his head until Landon dumped the items on the counter.

"Hurry up, dork." Bullying a kid went against Landon's nature and every principle he believed in, but to ensure Eja's protection, he needed to be remembered. "I don't have all night."

Saddened to see the teenager ring the transaction with his eyes cast down, Landon silently promised to come back and apologize.

"Don't ignore me when I'm talking to you." Landon slapped his credit card on the counter. "How much do hot babes cost in this crappy town?"

The teenager answered with a despondent shrug.

Relieved that the teenager wasn't aware of the hourly rate, Landon proceeded toward the back of the store. An ATM stood under the washroom sign.

He withdrew a thousand dollars.

* * *

Diffused light filtered through the ceiling of the cave. Although she couldn't see any gaps between the layers of rocks, there was no mistaking real sunlight.

Meg pressed a goblet against her mouth. "Drink, child."

She heard mumbled sounds that only made sense when she read them on Meg's lips. A hand palmed the base of her skull, tilting her head forward. Cold liquid moistened her parched lips. She gulped down a sip, then another. Water trickled down her throat and ran down her chin. She was thirsty, so thirsty.

"Drink slow." Smiling a kind, crooked smile, Meg eased the goblet back and forth to prevent her from choking. "It's empty. Would you like more?"

Still thirsty, she touched Meg's bony forearm. "Yes, please."

Meg lowered her head back onto a pillow, then walked to a table pushed against a stony wall. Made of antlers, the legs gave the table a rustic charm. A pitcher sat on top. Meg refilled the goblet from it.

Curious about her surroundings, Raven

110

propped herself on her elbows to sit upright. The bearskin slipped down her chest, exposing a pretty beige nightgown. A fox was embroidered over her left breast. She didn't remember the garment any more than the cave she slept in. *Where am I? How did I get here?*

A fire burned in a pit, warming up the cave. The flames spun around the room, and a wave of dizziness assailed her.

* * *

At the booth of the ferry station, Landon paid cash for two one-way tickets and a cabin.

The teller, an older lady with a strong accent, cast a fond gaze on the youngster fast asleep in his arms. "Cute little boy you have, sir."

The warm breath tickling Landon's neck kindled a yearning in his heart. "Thanks."

He boarded the ferry on foot and headed directly for his cabin. Hopefully, the teller would forget about Eja as soon as she laid eyes on another cute kid. The fewer people that Landon interacted with, the less likely he was to be remembered.

After tucking the boy into the left bed, Landon sat on the right one to write a letter. Once it was finished, he allowed himself to lie down and relax.

The wind rattled the windows, and the angry sea rocked the ferry.

His hands behind his head, he stared at the ceiling.

Eja was safe, and the phone call that Landon had made from the hospital ensured the boy would remain safe. Rusty's fate wasn't as certain, but her winter fur was thick, and she was resilient. The three-legged animal could probably survive a few days in the cold. Raven was the one sending the wheels in Landon's brain into a spinning frenzy.

His personal relationships had never lasted, mainly because duty had always come first. The fate of strangers took priority over birthday parties or dinner dates. Throughout his career, Landon had never given more than a passing thought to the possibility of having a wife, a child, or a dog. Raven had unwittingly exposed the void in his life and rekindled the dream that he didn't realize was hidden in the recesses of his heart.

Swayed by the sea, he dozed on and off until an announcement, drowned out by static, prompted him to get up.

Outside the window, the first ray of sunlight peeked over the ocean.

"Wake up, little man." Landon gently rubbed Eja's back, rousing him from a deep slumber. "We need to go to the bathroom, then it's time to disembark."

She slowly sat in bed. The throbbing in her skull and the dizziness weren't as pronounced as they were hours... or days ago.

Time had slipped away from her, meeting the same fate as her memory. With cautious fingers, she probed the back of her head. A bandage covered the sore area. "How bad is it?"

"The bleeding stopped, and the wound isn't infected. It will heal." Along with a reassuring smile, Meg offered her a steamy cup. "Drink this."

The broth smelled delicious.

"Who am I? What happened to me?" The fire in the cave burned in silence, and yet she clearly remembered the crackling and popping sounds associated with it. "Why can't I hear properly?" *Instead of feeling like my head is underwater and I'm drowning in confusion.*

"I don't know who you are, but fate kept you alive."

On the lips of the older woman, the word fate resembled a blessing. "Fate seems like a nice name."

"Fate?" Twinkles sparkled in Meg's dark eyes. "It fits you. You were alone in the forest when two men attacked you. One hit you on the head with a big stick. It's probably why you can't remember or hear everything."

"Those two men…" The blurry image of a man with dark brown eyes lingered at the edge of her mind. "Do you know why they attacked me? Did they say anything?"

"No, but five years ago, I saw them kill a white elder in the forest." A strand of salt and pepper hair escaped Meg's ponytail and dangled in front of her eyes. "Late yesterday morning, I stumbled onto them while I checked my traps. They were hiding near where the river splits in two. It looked as if they were waiting for you."

Cold invaded Fate's body. "Won't they find me here?"

"No." Meg patted Fate's knee over the bearskin. "You were fleeing on your snowmobile when the bigger guy hit you. You slumped against the windshield, steering toward the trees where I was hiding. I hopped on and rode away with you. One of them followed. I knew he would catch up with us, so I crashed into a beaver lodge and tossed your parka on the seat. Your snowmobile sank within minutes. I erased the traces leading away from the crash and took you across the beaver dam. No one followed us here."

"You saved my life and staged my death?" *I have no more past.* That was one clever and ironic twist if Fate could hear one.

"I didn't want them to keep searching for you. When you're strong and ready, you can resurface. Now rest, Fate. Your mind and body need to heal."

* * *

Holding tight to the little hand tucked in his, Landon searched the parking lot of the ferry terminal.

In the last row, next to a dark green SUV, his father waved at him.

Landon picked up Eja and hurried toward him. "Thanks for coming, Pa."

"Did I have a choice?" teased his father. "I found a car seat, like you requested, and your sister installed it. I'm guessing it's for you, Eja." Papa Steele pulled out a blue teddy bear from behind his back. "A gift from Auntie Charlotte. She's baking chocolate chip cookies, waiting for you."

His father doted on his three grandchildren, all blessings from Landon's only sibling, Charlotte, and her husband, Oliver. To see his family welcome Eja in their loving fold warmed Landon's heart and put his mind at ease. His little man would not only be safe with them, but he would also be loved.

The boy hesitantly took the bear and hugged it to his chest.

Landon cupped Eja's cheek, gently stroking it with his thumb. "This is my father. His name is Papa. He will take care of you while I search for your mother."

Silent tears brimmed in Eja's eyes.

"I will come back for you, little man. I promise." Landon kissed the boy's forehead, then buckled him up in the car seat. "Hold on to your new bear, and don't let Papa, Auntie Charlotte, or Uncle Oliver spoil you too much, okay?"

Heartened by the faint smile on Eja's lips, Landon closed the back door.

"Why do I have the feeling you're *not* coming with us?" Papa Steele stood by the driver's door, his hand on the handle. "Are you going to tell me what's really going on, son?"

After blindly following the directives that Landon had given him over the phone, his father deserved an explanation.

"I believe Eja witnessed the vicious beating of an RCMP officer. The trauma stole his voice. He needs to be protected at all costs. You, Charlotte, and Oliver are the only people I trust right now. For everyone's safety, you must stay under the radar and avoid contacting me. I'm reboarding the ferry so I can search for his mom. She's gone missing after an explosion." Landon handed him the letter that he had written on the ferry. "It may take me a while. These are instructions in case... you know."

Papa Steele nodded. As a recently retired fire chief, he understood duty and risks. "We'll keep him safe and wait for you at the cottage—for as long as it takes."

                    * * *

A fair-skinned child ran toward her, arms wide open and tears brimming in his beautiful blue eyes. Pain wrenched Fate's heart. She had never seen such innocent eyes reflecting so much suffering.

An axe tumbled from the top of a majestic fir tree, chopping a snowy branch in its descent. No taller than a sapling, the child stilled and looked up.

No! Fate snapped her eyes open, instantly awoken. The nightmare faded away before the youngster suffered any harm. "Who are you?"

Something touched her arm, startling her.

Meg retrieved her hand but kept staring at her. Worries obscured her face. "Bad dream?"

"I'm always seeing the same child bundled in a snowsuit. I think it's a boy." The image was genderless, but when he reached for her, Fate felt like she knew him. "He has gorgeous blue eyes."

A smile softened Meg's expression. "You have blue eyes. Maybe you're seeing yourself."

"I doubt that." Fate's long hair was pitch black, and her skin was as dark as Meg's. *Indigenous blood has to flow through my veins.* "The child was white. I'm not. What do I look like? How old do you think I am?"

"Indigenous, pretty, late twenties." Meg smiled. "I wish I had a mirror."

Me too. "I remember the difference between a bear and a moose pelt but not who I am." Or who the child was, but she nonetheless felt a connection between them. "How far are we from where I was attacked?"

"About three hours from the main entrance."

The answer suggested the cave possessed more than one opening. "Any other exits?"

"Yes, but it leads in the opposite direction." Meg's gaze wandered to a corner of the cave where sunlight seeped through a gap in the ceiling. "I carried you through it. Your snowmobile is buried forty minutes away."

"Are you saying you walk everywhere?"

Meg hadn't mentioned any mode of transportation, but she obviously wandered around.

"My snowshoes don't need fuel, they don't make noise, and if I drag a branch behind me, I can easily erase my prints. As long as I can check my traps and return before nightfall, I don't need an engine."

Many questions swirled inside Fate's mind, but she had more pressing issues to deal with than indulging her curiosity about the reasons that prompted Meg to live in a cave. "Do we have time to return to the crash site? I'd like to see my snowmobile."

The dubious look on Meg's face

conveyed her surprise. "It's at the bottom of the pond. There's nothing to see, except maybe for a few angry beavers."

"Please?" Fate didn't feel strong enough for a three-hour trek to the site of her attack, but she should be able to manage an eighty-minute round trip to the pond. "It may joggle my memory."

"I suppose some exercise can't hurt." Meg rummaged through the cave, visibly displeased, then handed her some warm clothes and a pair of snowshoes. "You'll need this."

In awe of the snowshoes' craftsmanship, Fate stroked the rabbit paws tied at the back. Fleeting images she couldn't capture flickered through her mind. "Did you make these?"

"No, they belonged to the white elder. His attackers untied his snowshoes and tossed them among the trees. Maybe they didn't want him to escape, not that it mattered at the end. He didn't need his snowshoes to enter the spirit world, so I kept them. Now, get dressed. I will tell you more about him and the three men who killed him later."

Chapter 8

Landon peeked at his phone through heavy eyelids and groaned. *7 a.m.*

Exhausted, he dragged himself out of bed. Another knock resonated in the house, echoing in his skull.

He nabbed the knob and yanked the door open. "Bloody hell, what do you—" Upon seeing his sergeant, Landon swallowed *want.*

Beck glared at him, his face flushed. "Did you even bother sobering up before you drove back?"

Not drunk, just overtired. Same symptoms but different causes. As long as Beck didn't charge him for drinking and driving, Landon welcomed the misconception. "What makes you think I drove anywhere?"

"Don't take me for an idiot." Beck elbowed his way in and kicked the door shut with his boot. "Two days ago, you went AWOL, filled up for gas in Port aux Basques, withdrew a thousand bucks from an ATM, booked a cheap motel with your credit card, and squandered your money on hookers. We

120

talked to the gas station and motel attendants. They remember you, Steele.”

At Port aux Basques, Landon had parked his Jeep behind a sleazy motel near the ferry terminal, used his credit card to pay for a room, inquired about hookers, emptied his cans of beer and tomato juice in the sink before leaving them on the floor, ruffled the sheet and towels, and hung the *Do-Not-Disturb* sign on the doorknob. Then, while no one was in the vicinity of the parking lot, Landon had scooped the boy from his Jeep and carried him to the ferry terminal.

Landon had made certain his trail ended at that motel, and Eja remained invisible in case someone at the detachment kept tabs on his whereabouts. *I was right to be careful.* “Should have paid cash,” he mumbled to protect his whereabouts. “It was the anniversary of my mother’s death. I needed to get away. Can I go back to sleep now?”

“No.” His sergeant wandered inside the living room, gazing around. “Caleb Marshall came in yesterday afternoon. He was looking for you.”

“What did he want?” In his exhausted state, it didn’t take Landon much effort to pretend he was clueless.

“His sister’s cabin blew up, and she and her boy are missing.” The lack of emotion in Beck’s voice rubbed Landon the wrong way. “Caleb is worried.”

Someone blew up her cabin, Beck. Of course her brother is worried. A red flag would flap in Landon's mind if Caleb wasn't. "Did someone search the debris? Did you establish the cause of the blast?"

"No human remains were found on the site." Beck eyed him. "The preliminary report points to the propane tank as the cause of the explosion."

The wave of relief washing over Landon receded as quickly as it had rolled in. Raven loved her son. She would never have intentionally abandoned him. Something had prevented her from coming home, and that something didn't bode well for her safety. "A propane tank?"

"An inspector already visited the site of the explosion." Beck's gaze wandered toward the fireplace. "He suspects a defective safety valve."

Anyone can tamper with a safety valve and make an explosion look like an accident. Learning how the perp blew up the cabin didn't help narrowing Landon's list of suspects. "Who's in charge of the investigation?"

"You are, so don't think about jumping off the deep end like Harrison." His sergeant backtracked into the kitchen. "The faster you investigate the explosion and get Caleb off my back, the sooner I'll forget about your unauthorized escapade."

* * *

Fate snowshoed toward the site of her attack, pondering the tragic story of the white elder.

The account of his attack resonated in her bones. With each step she took through the snow, the rabbit paws bounced behind her, stirring a warm feeling. They had faced the same monsters, and though they met different fates, Fate felt the elderly man's spirit inside her.

Meg paused near a frozen river. "The two men ambushed you here."

A recent snowfall had erased any trace of the violent encounter. The site didn't yield any more memories than the damaged beaver lodge she had seen a few days earlier. "How far are we from the nearest town?"

"A full day of walking, maybe more, but there are lots of cabins in the forest." Meg pointed east. "The white elder lived that way."

"Did you ever contact his family?" A disturbing thought crossed Fate's mind. Justice hadn't been served, or else the elder's killers would be in jail, paying for their crime, not on the loose, free to attack her. "Meg, did you ever give a description of his killers to the police?"

"I've never met his family, and I sure never went to the Mounties. They would have arrested me and framed me for Arnie's death, like they framed two dead indigenous kids for his death. I saw their bodies, Fate.

Neither kid was as skinny as the smallest attacker. You can't trust the police. Women like us don't get justice." A look of panic flitted across Meg's face. "I hear an engine. Hurry, we must hide."

* * *

Landon could only speculate as to why he was put in charge of the investigation. Whatever the reason, it gave him the opportunity to snoop around Raven's cabin without raising suspicion.

Rusty? Where are you, girl? The dog was nowhere in sight. *Did you get scared and hide in the forest like Raven?*

With all the different people who visited the explosion site in the last few days and the snowfall from last night, any prints or evidence worth gathering had either been collected or buried.

I glimpsed a potential suspect. It can't be a coincidence or an accident.

Disappointed by his fruitless search of the explosion site, Landon entered the coordinates he had copied from her grandfather's and Harrison's police files into his snowmobile GPS. *These are the locations where the bodies of Raven's grandfather and Abbot were recovered.*

Back at the detachment, Landon had seen the photos of the old crime scenes, but he wanted to see the locations and the surrounding areas with his own eyes.

Besides, Raven is somewhere in the forest. There were many places where she could go for a snowmobile ride, but these were the only two sites he could think of that she might want to revisit alone. *Why didn't I inquire about your destination when you let me look at your computer?*

He plowed through the fresh layer of snow, the oversight eating at him. The naked deciduous trees shivered in the cold, surrounded by snowy evergreens. The beautiful landscape changed little the farther he rode, but as magnificent as the forest was, it could also bring death to any rider lost in its cold embrace.

A dot bleeped on the screen of the GPS.

This is it, I guess. He stopped his vehicle near a huge boulder and scrutinized the area.

Five years had passed since Raven's grandfather met a tragic fate here, and yet the landscape shared an uncanny resemblance with the crime scene photos. *Minus the body and the blood.*

No lair. No hangout. Nothing stood out.

Why would anyone kill an elderly man who was out checking his traps? A thief? But why was he found without his snowshoes?

Frustrated by the lack of answers, Landon let his gaze wander across the peaceful scenery, catching sight of smudgy impressions in the snow between two large trees.

Intrigued, he strapped his snowshoes and marched on.

Swayed by the wind, the low branches brushed snow into a series of fresh snowshoe prints zigzagging between the trees.

Someone was here not long ago. Adrenaline rushed through his body, heightening his senses.

A branch cracked behind him.

Landon spun around. Something struck him behind the knees. He tumbled forward. Hurried steps crunched in the snow. He looked up.

Two women wearing fur clothes snowshoed away.

Despite the pain searing up his legs, Landon staggered up.

Aside from the walking stick one of them carried, they appeared unarmed. Had the one who hit him mustered more strength, she could have incapacitated him.

The women disappeared amid the trees.

Bloody hell, they're fast. Through the branches, he measured their progress as he gave chase.

The woman with the stick led the way, her steps short and brisk, while the one behind gracefully skidded over the snow.

"RCMP! Stop!" With his longer stride, he gained on them. "I said stop!"

The woman farther ahead motioned for her accomplice to hurry.

Landon was at a loss to explain what they could be doing snowshoeing deep in the forest so far from town, but they obviously perceived him as a threat, or else they wouldn't have hit him and fled. "I just want to talk!"

Fallen trees and scratchy shrubs hindered their escape, and the gap between him and them shrank to less than fifteen feet. The leading woman skipped over a dead tree. The other followed suit. One of her snowshoes caught on a branch. She tumbled onto her hands and knees.

"Fate! Get up!"

Seizing his chances, Landon lunged forward and tackled the one named Fate into the snow. He landed on top, grasping her wrists. Kicking and thrashing, she swung her head left and right. He tightened his grip. "Stop!"

"Let go of me." She stilled and glared at him in defiance.

Thunderstruck by her blue eyes, he pushed himself up. "Ra—"

Blackness embraced him.

* * *

Fate understood mistrust. Not remembering who she could and couldn't trust only amplified the feeling. Until she recovered her memory, she wasn't inclined to trust anyone, but she drew a line at indifference.

"We can't abandon him in the forest, Meg." *His life matters.* "If we leave him and he doesn't regain consciousness, he'll die of exposure." *I can't have his death on my conscience.*

"If we stay here and he regains conscious, we'll get arrested." Meg kicked snow in his direction. "I'm going home. Are you coming?"

The officer's haunted expression when he had looked at her, seconds before Meg hit him, was etched on Fate's memory. It was like he had seen a ghost, and she was that ghost. "Would you help me? Please?"

Meg turned around and snowshoed away. If she said anything, Fate didn't hear her.

Swell... Fate stared at the officer lying in the snow. He was out cold but still breathing. *You better not make me regret doing the right thing.*

Knowing she couldn't carry his dead weight through the snow, Raven searched his pocket for a key or a fob to start his snowmobile. She found two fobs. Unsure which one she needed, she pocketed both, brought the vehicle to him, then dragged him into its sled.

Hoping to bring him back near where he came from, Raven rode back into his tracks until she reached a battered shed next to the ruins of what might have been a cabin. *Something bad happened here.*

She parked by the shed. Its door swung

open. A three-legged German Shepherd came out, its tail wagging, and scrambled to nuzzle Raven's leg.

"Hi, buddy." Raven petted the friendly animal. "What are you doing here alone? Are you waiting for someone?"

The dog bounced toward the sled, stopping by the officer's head.

"Does the officer belong to you?" Pleased to see the dog lick the officer's face, Fate smiled. "If I give him back to you, will you keep him warm until he wakes up?"

Under the watchful eye of the dog, Fate dragged the officer into the shed where she propped his back against a set of tires. The dog lay down next to his legs.

"You're a good dog." Fate rubbed the dog's back. Its fur was thick and healthy. Despite its missing leg, the animal looked well taken care of. "The officer is treating you right, isn't he? You stay and take good care of him."

Its ears pricked, the dog lowered its head on the officer's lap.

Fate closed the door of the shed, then rode the officer's snowmobile back to where the river split in two. Once there, she disabled the engine and his radio to make it look like he had run into trouble, tossed both fobs in the hidden compartment under the seat, and snowshoed away.

* * *

Something licked his face. Something warm and wet. Landon snapped his eyes open, quickly moving a hand to his face. "Rusty?"

The dog curled up on his lap.

"I'm happy to see you too, girl. Are you hurt?" He checked her for injuries, finding no signs of any. Thankfully, he scratched her behind the ears. "Where have you been?"

His gaze wandered through the mayhem around him. "And where are we?"

He sat inside a ransacked shack, his snowshoes still strapped to his boots and his back against a pile of tires. Vestiges of his encounter in the forest emerged from his throbbing head. "Raven?"

Unsure if he should trust his memory, he touched the back of his head and winced. A lump the size of a hockey puck protruded from his skull. *I didn't dream the attack*. It was real, which meant Raven was alive.

Relief should wash over him, not add a heavier weight on his shoulders. "What possessed you to flee with the woman who hit me twice?"

The sun shining through a broken window cast a yellow hue on the knocked-down shelves, damaged tools, dented cans, and shattered glass. Still, Raven's bizarre behaviour remained shrouded in mystery.

Rusty nibbled on his glove, her paw

130

resting on his holster. He checked his gun and his pockets. His fobs were missing. *That can't be good.* He nudged Rusty sideways and slowly stood. "Let's try getting out of here."

The door was closed.

Landon pushed it and took a step outside. A gasp of consternation escaped his mouth.

Through the misty white cloud drifting in front of his eyes, he gazed at the ruins of Raven's cabin.

"Bloody hell, how did I end up here?" *And where's my snowmobile?*

* * *

Fate approached the entrance of Meg's cave. "Meg, are you there?" The older woman kept knives, and Fate didn't want to startle her by entering unannounced. "I'm coming in."

Crouched by the fire, Meg glared at her while stirring the embers with a stick. "What did you do with him?"

The frosty welcome chilled Fate. *I'll have nowhere else to go before nightfall if Meg decides to kick me out.* "He's cooped up with a big dog in a shed near some ruins in a clearing."

The older woman retreated toward the back of the cave, her feelings toward the officer as visible as the flames keeping the cave warm. "What about his snowmobile?"

"I abandoned it by the river and was careful to cover my tracks as I snowshoed back here." Fate had ensured that taking him to safety didn't come at the risk of leading anyone to Meg's cave. "I didn't place you in danger."

"Maybe not, but you disobeyed my wishes." Meg picked up a hunting knife from the top of a rain barrel and ran a hand over the blade. "It takes a great dose of courage to do what you did today." With a swift blow, she jabbed the knife into the barrel. "I have none left, but there's still hope for you."

* * *

After spending hours looking for his snowmobile, only to find it with Beck's help near the frozen river, Landon drove into town, where he stopped at the pet shop to buy a bag of food.

Once Rusty settled down in his kitchen in front of two bowls, one filled with water and the other with kibbles, Landon walked to the detachment, still baffled by the latest events.

The front door opened.

Harrison's widow walked out. Wrapped in a fur coat, she added her boot prints to the few imprinted in the fresh layer of snow covering the walkway. "Corporal Steele, I heard about your misadventure in the forest today." A cross between disdain and suspicion swirled in her mystic green eyes. "Anyone with an ounce of common sense would have looked under the hood of his snowmobile after it stalled, not abandoned it with the fob under the seat, but I suppose it's too much to ask from someone who doesn't bother looking at his watch before waking up a grieving family."

Unsure what prompted her to rehash their earliest encounter, Landon shrugged at the insult. "I'm not a mechanic, ma'am." However, he was impressed that Beck managed to fix whatever had been disabled, saving them the trouble of towing the snowmobile. "Have a good day."

She left in a silver Lexus while Landon quickly shovelled the walkway. Once he finished, he returned the shovel next to the door and entered.

"If it isn't our expert navigator." Tobin leaned back in his chair, his sleeves rolled up to his elbows. "Let me see if I got this straight. Your engine stalled in the forest and your radio went silent, so you tossed your fob under the seat for anyone to steal, snowshoed back until you got a cell signal but tumbled along the way, bumped your head, got disoriented, ended up in Raven's shed, and forgot where you abandoned your snowmobile in the first place. Did I miss anything?"

Tobin had recounted almost word for word the cover story that Landon had fed his sergeant. "Beck didn't leave out any details, did he? Do I want to know what compelled you to share my misadventure with Harrison's widow?"

"Alessi was here thanking me for Lyn's train when Beck returned and spilled the beans." A peculiar expression settled over Tobin's face. "The sarge was peeved he wasted hours searching for your snowmobile while you tagged along with Raven's beast in his sled. He couldn't believe you didn't notice you'd stalled near the big boulder. That's a landmark, Steele. What were you doing there anyway?"

Why are you asking about my whereabouts? "I was following paw prints in the snow," Landon lied, maintaining his best poker face. "Don't I get some credits for finding Rusty?"

"The doc won't care much that you found the beast alive, but not his sister or nephew. You know there's a reason why Beck put you in charge of this investigation, right? He knows they're dead, so when their bodies resurface, the fingers will be pointing at you for not finding them in time. Beck will wash his hands of you and go on enjoying his retirement."

"Is that so?" *If you believe that's how the chain of command works, Tobin, I pity the men and women who may one day end up under your command.* "If it's all the same to you, I'll assume they're alive until proven otherwise. Do we have a list of people living off the land and under the radar in the forest?"

"No but…" His colleague furrowed his brows. "There are lots of dangerous animals living in the forest, Steele. Be careful poking the ones that don't walk on all fours."

You're right. Some walk on twos and wear uniforms. Landon had come to work to glean information on the mysterious woman fleeing with Raven, not to discover more flaws in Tobin's character. "I'm going to see the doc. I need something to shrink the bump on my head."

* * *

Seated on the cold slab in the morgue, Landon winced under the doctor's examination. "I'm fine, Doc. The bump was just an excuse to come see you. We need to talk off the record about your sister."

"I heard a faulty valve caused the propane tank to explode." Caleb pulled a chair from underneath the counter and straddled it. "It's my fault. I knew the cabin was old, and it wasn't safe for Raven to live there alone with Eja. I built a basement suite in my new house just for them. I can afford to support them, but Raven won't move in. I should have insisted. I—" His elbows hit the

135

edge of the backrest. "Why didn't she listen?"

"Because she's a proud, resourceful, and fiercely independent woman?" *The kind of woman who can haunt a man for the rest of his life.* "There were no bodies on the site of the explosion. No one died in the clearing, and I found Rusty today, famished but alive. If a three-legged animal managed to survive, the odds your sister found shelter in the forest are very much in her favour, don't you think?" Disguising the truth brought Landon no satisfaction. It only added to his burden, but to protect Raven's family, he couldn't reveal their whereabouts yet. "I won't stop looking for them. That's a promise, Doc, but I need your help."

Caleb stared at him with a faraway look in his eyes. "From the day Gramp brought me and Raven home to his cabin, he taught us survival skills. I never paid as much attention as I should have, but Raven..." The shadow of a smile flitted across the doctor's face. "There was nothing she couldn't or didn't learn. You're right about the odds. Raven and Eja are somewhere out there. How can I help?"

Glad to see the fog of guilt or despair dissipate over Caleb's head, Landon bolted off the table. "Did Raven ever talk to you about the day she found your grandfather?"

"Not really, but..." Caleb heaved a long breath. "A few days ago, she came to see me out of the blue. She wanted to look at the autopsy reports of Gramp and the two teenagers who killed him."

The timing unsettled Landon. If she had been suspicious of her grandfather's death before he showed her the suicide note, it was possible she had asked one too many questions and threatened the murderers. *It could spell motive to eliminate her.* "Did she say why?"

"No, and I refused her request. She wasn't too happy." As her brother, Caleb could have told her about their grandfather, but as a medical examiner, he was bound by confidentiality regarding the teenagers.

"I noticed your sister isn't too fond of no as an answer, but I would like to see those reports." Landon had read their grandfather's report but not the boys'. "And I won't take no for an answer."

Caleb chuckled, pointing at a filing cabinet next to a water cooler. "Help yourself."

On top of the cabinet, a miniature skeleton dangled from the hook of a banana holder. Landon read the label above each handle. First drawer: A-H. He opened it and looked for Nelson Bourke's file. Once he retrieved it, he searched for Percy Foley's.

In the Fs, Landon stumbled onto Noel Foley's autopsy report. *What are you doing there, Noel?* In Noel's police report, there had been no mention of his death. *When did you kick the bucket?*

Landon pulled Noel's file along with his cousin Percy's, then browsed through Noel's report first.

You died of a single gunshot to the heart on November 18th. If Landon's memory served him well, Noel Foley was arrested by Harrison on November 10th. *That's a week after your arrest. And a week later, Harrison met the same fate.* The coincidence didn't sit well with Landon, who kept flipping through the pages.

The toxicology had shown an elevated blood alcohol level. Caleb had signed the autopsy report.

"Doc, does the name Noel Foley ring a bell?" Landon waved the report in the air. "According to this, you dislodged a bullet from his heart last November."

"Noel cleaned his loaded rifle while he was drunk. Clive, his neighbour from across the pond, heard the shot. By the time he reached Noel's cabin, it was too late." The doctor pulled his stethoscope from around his neck. "The bloody rag in Foley's hand was sent to the lab, and two sets of DNA were recovered. Foley's and an identified male. The age testing of the blood, which proves accurate seventy per cent of the time, indicated both men stained the rag at around the same time. I don't know how much of an investigation your colleagues did, but his death was ruled accidental. His cousin Percy was one of the teenagers who killed Gramp."

Whoever investigated the accidental shooting should have left a paper trail. However, Landon had found none. His suspicion rose another notch. "Was Noel's cabin near Raven's?"

"No, not at all. Opposite direction from town. Noel had no family left. His cabin is probably abandoned by now." Caleb tossed the stethoscope on the counter. "Why?"

"Not sure yet..." *Sniffing around Noel's cabin may reveal clues that were missed in November.*

Chapter 9

Fate woke up in a cold cave. The fire had died sometime during the night, and no one had woken up to rekindle it.

Wrapped in a pelt, Fate kneeled by the other woman's bed. "Meg?"

The older woman lay on her back, her eyes closed and her expression serene.

Hoping to rouse her, Fate shook her hand, a hand as cold as ice.

"No, no, no..." Fate checked for pulse. When she found none, she placed an open palm next to Meg's mouth. No breath of air tingled Fate's skin. "You can't be dead."

Tears of despair, anger, and sorrow pooled in her eyes, blurring her vision.

Fleeting images of different bodies overlaid Meg's. "Who are you?" The answers lurked at the edge of Fate's subconscious and then vanished in the blink of an eye. Bewildered, she wiped away her tears. "Are you spirits? Or memories?"

Unsettled by both possibilities, Fate rose to her feet. She couldn't let Meg rot in this cave any more than she could throw her dead body in the snow. "You deserve a proper burial." In the summer, Fate could have dug a real grave, but not in winter. "I need to take you somewhere you'll be found and not eaten by animals."

After rekindling the fire and eating breakfast, Fate collected three strong dead branches of roughly six feet long. She bent the twigs growing from them. Most growths snapped instantly, but a few required a fair amount of twisting and pulling. She then broke the longest branch in half.

"I have two long poles and two short crossbars." She didn't remember who taught her how to make an improvised stretcher, but she remembered the instructions in vivid detail. "Next, I need a jacket."

She inverted the sleeves of Meg's fur coat so they ran along the inside of the coat, then threaded the poles through the sleeves. To keep the coat taut and add stability to the stretcher, she tied a crossbar at each end using the leather bindings of an old pair of snowshoes.

"The stretcher is ready, Meg. It's time for you to leave the cave and return to civilization."

* * *

On his way to Noel's cabin, Landon rode over many animal prints. As he approached, a red fox dashed in front of his snowmobile, prompting him to stop near an outhouse.

The roof of Noel's cabin had caved in, creating a safety hazard to anyone trying to get in, but it hadn't stopped foxes from turning it into a den.

It doesn't look like I'll be gleaning any new information here. Landon circled the cabin once to ascertain he didn't miss anything, then rode across the pond to where Noel's neighbour lived.

Landon knocked on the door. "Wake up, Clive. The sun is up."

The door opened a few inches, baring a greyish man in his mid-fifties. "Come back with a warrant. I'm sleeping."

"I'm giving you three choices, Clive. You can answer my questions either outside, in your cabin, or at the detachment." Hoping to rattle his witness, Landon placed a gloved hand on his holster. "I strongly suggest you pick the right choice and let me come in."

The man backed away from the door, grumbling. Landon stepped in, closed the door, and lowered his hand. The bare-chested man wore a pair of long yellowish johns that left little to the imagination and concealed no weapon.

"Have a seat on the couch, Clive."

The man sneered, complying. "What do you want?"

Glad to skip the pleasantries, Landon stood with his back to the door. "Last November, you found Noel's body in his cabin. Do you recall that day?"

"I try not to." Clive grabbed the flask propped against the armrest. "Why?"

"Talk me through what happened that day, would you?" Landon crossed his arms over his chest in a not-so-subtle hint that he wasn't leaving until he got the entire story.

"I'd gone hunting with him that morning, but we didn't fire a single bullet. He was my only neighbour, and he had no family left, not since his cousin's death, so I kinda took him under my wing. A few hours later, I heard a gunshot. I wanted to know what he'd killed, so I went to see him." Clive took a swig from his flask. "I found him sitting on the floor near the fireplace, his rifle on his lap, a dirty rag in his hand, and a bloody hole in his chest. I called you guys right away."

Noel didn't fire any shots, but he still cleaned his rifle and managed to kill himself? That sounds too convenient. "Did you see anyone lurking around Noel's cabin that day? Was there any booze near his body?"

"'Course he died with a bottle. He hadn't been sober since the day he was born." Clive took another swig. "And no, I didn't see anyone else."

That's unfortunate. "When you found Noel, did you notice anything unusual? Anything that made you pause?"

"I've watched him clean his rifle many times. He always checked twice to make sure it wasn't loaded. Didn't matter how drunk he was. Maybe he didn't look too closely..." Clive rubbed his stubbly chin. "Come to think of it, the rag was in his right hand. He was a lefty. That was weird, but the bottle was in his left. Maybe he was drinking more than he was cleaning."

The inconsistency bothered Landon. "Did you share your observations with the officer in charge of investigating his death?"

"And get involved? Are you kidding?" The man glared at him. "I don't trust any of you, not after what Noel told me."

Trust me, Clive, I get the trust issue. "And what did Noel say?"

"He said someone killed and framed his cousin for murder." Clive's voice rose. "He said he could prove it, but you wouldn't listen."

The report Harrison taped under his seat proved he'd listened to Noel. And they both conveniently ended up dead. "I'm listening now, Clive."

"You're too late." The man slumped on the couch. "Noel took whatever proof he had to his grave."

* * *

Fate trekked through the forest, pulling the stretcher behind her. The woman who had saved her life rested on the fur coat, covered from hair to boots with a bear pelt.

Birds that Fate could see but not hear flew between the branches. Their presence soothed her troubled mind. Hours on end, she trudged through the snow, afraid she might not be able to resume her grueling procession if she stopped even for an instant.

The muscles in her legs stiffened, the leather straps she pulled cut through her mittens, her lungs burned, her lips were parched, and her mouth was dry. The sun's progression across the sky was her only bearing. Meg had mentioned cabins in the forest, lots of cabins, but Fate had yet to stumble onto one.

Exhausted and disheartened, she struggled to keep moving one foot after the other.

No smoke danced in the blue sky, but in the distance, a red roof peeked through the needles of the evergreens. The light breeze only carried the fresh, crispy aroma of winter, not the scent of burning woods.

A small clearing opened in front of her, revealing a ramshackle log cabin. Traces of snow grazed its steep red roof, but feet of snow had accumulated around the exterior walls, reaching the ledge of a broken window and concealing the latch on the door.

No one will find Meg if I abandon her here. Then again, no one will find me either. The abandoned cabin provided Fate with a safe place to rest.

She left the stretcher underneath the window and then trekked around the cabin looking for a more accessible door.

On the right side, two frosty windows framed the round metal chimney rising above the roof. The presence of a chimney implied the presence of a stove in the cabin, and a stove meant heat throughout the night.

The back of the cabin consisted of a full wall, but some twenty feet behind stood a shed with a flat roof, its crooked door ajar. Near the latch, a handle peeked from the snow. Fate grabbed the handle and pulled, extracting a shovel.

Meg's body would attract predators if left outside for the night, but it would start decomposing if Fate brought it inside and lit a fire.

I could hide Meg's body in the shed. It would stay frozen without becoming prey.

Fate cleared the snow in front of the shed and then pulled on the latch. The upper hinge gave way suddenly and the door grazed her shoulder swinging down. The other hinge broke. The door landed in the snow amid a cloud of flurries.

Grateful she avoided serious injuries, Fate looked inside the shed. It was empty except for a big hole in the corner of its hard-packed dirt floor.

The shed would protect Meg's body from the coyotes or lynx. *I just need to get that door upright, but first I need to start a fire and rest for a few minutes.*

                    * * *

Landon rode through the forest pondering Noel's death. His path crossed an unusual trail, prompting him to stop. The flattened trail, smudged with ill-defined snowshoe prints, ran between two parallel lines.

"Someone is dragging something across the forest." More suspicious of the *who* and the *what* than the *why*, Landon followed the trail to a cabin with a red roof.

A stretcher was abandoned in the snow near the window.

Anticipating more trouble, Landon parked alongside it.

Someone appeared to lie on the stretcher underneath a black pelt. Landon lifted a corner and sucked in a sharp breath of cold air. *You're Raven's aggressive sidekick.* The older woman's eyes were closed, and her skin was blue, but he still recognized her right away. *How did you end up dead?*

Something clunked inside the cabin.

Landon removed his helmet, straining his ears as he approached the cabin. The front door was ajar. Through the gap, he spied firewood being tossed in a woodstove. He shouldered the door open and drew his gun, stepping in.

"RCMP! Don't move!" He laid eyes on the intruder and stopped dead in his tracks. There was no mistaking her, even from behind. He holstered his weapon and waited for Raven to sense his presence.

She rummaged through the drawers and cupboards. A pair of snowshoes with traces of snow on them rested against the leg of a wooden table. Landon counted three chairs, all broken. A handle snapped, and a drawer dropped onto the floor, scattering utensils amid shards of broken dishes. Raven turned sideways, stepping back.

Their gaze met, and she stilled.

"Meg died in her sleep." The quivering in her voice heightened her melodious accent. "I just wanted someone to find her and bury her."

"I wasn't accusing you, Raven." The frightened look in her eyes unsettled him. "I've been looking all—"

A noisy engine, growing louder by the second, disrupted their eerie encounter.

Landon glanced through the open door. A RCMP snowmobile zoomed through the landscape, heading toward the cabin.

"Raven, you're in grave danger. You need to hide." He shoved the snowshoes with the rabbit paws into her arms. "Hold on to them and don't make a sound."

Visibly aghast, she hugged them against her chest.

"We'll get through this, Raven. I promise." He scanned the cabin for a hiding place.

The cupboards weren't deep enough. The storage box had no lid. A gutted mattress lay in a corner near a slanted couch. He tossed a cushion on the floor to check its bottom. The cushion landed near an iron ring pinned to the floor.

"Come with me." His gloved hand spooning her bent elbow, Landon directed her toward the hardware sticking out inches away from the couch. He grabbed the ring and pulled. The hinges of the trapdoor creaked, and a gaping hole appeared at their feet.

A ladder descended into a dark cellar.

Raven recoiled. Afraid she might bolt, Landon cupped her face. Confusion swirled in her beautiful eyes.

With his glove, he couldn't feel her cheek. Still, he imagined her skin to be soft and warm. "You need to go down and stay quiet until I get you."

Somewhere in the back of his mind, he registered the silence surrounding the cabin.

"Go. Now." He kissed her forehead, nudged her down, then closed the trap. *Bloody hell, Steele, a kiss?* Mystified by his own action, he retreated to the kitchen.

Tobin barged in. "Steele? What are you doing here?"

I could ask you the same question. "I was searching abandoned cabins in case Raven and her son found shelter in one of them."

"The boy wouldn't have walked this far." His colleague roamed around the cabin. "There's a dead woman outside. Someone dragged her here, but I only see your snowmobile tracks outside."

I'm not welcoming your observations, Tobin. "The person fled before I arrived," Landon lied to prevent his colleague from snooping around. "I didn't realize I was riding in his trail until it was too late. Trust me, I wouldn't have erased the traces he left behind if I'd known I would find a dead body."

"If you say so..." Tobin paced in front of the couch. "No one's lived here in a long time. Why dump her body here?"

"How should I know? I'm not a mind reader. Why don't you help me carry her body into my sled, then you and I can process the scene." By asking for help, Landon hoped to chase Tobin away.

"Finders keepers, Steele. She's—" Tobin tripped over the trap ring and fell to his knees. "What the heck?"

His colleague lifted the trap before Landon could stop him. Silently cursing his bad luck, Landon switched to damage control mode. "Tobin, I should have—"

"Yeah, you should have warned me." Tobin slammed the trap shut, then kicked the side of the couch, sending dust swirling in the air. "I could have broken a leg, Steele. The body is all yours. Have fun screwing up that case too."

***

Unable to hear or see anything in the low cellar, Fate crawled on all fours, feeling her way forward with her hands, careful not to disturb anything or make any detectible sounds.

A pungent odour assaulted her nostrils and a draft of cold air pricked her cheeks. She followed the breeze, ending behind the ladder without having touched anything on the floor. Though it smelled of rotten food, the cellar felt empty. She ran a hand along the wall and stumbled onto a hole, a large hole by the feel of it. *Large enough for me to hide in it.*

She crawled into it, extending her arm to determine its depth. When she didn't touch any end wall, she probed farther and farther. *It's not a hole, it's a tunnel. And most tunnels have entrances at both ends.* Hoping that tunnel wasn't an exception to the rule, she kept advancing.

The officer had called her by a name that Fate didn't quite catch. *He knows me and seems to care, or else he wouldn't have kissed me.*

She had sensed his fears when he urged her to hide. Something he saw through the open door had brought it on. For their sake, she needed to remain as quiet as possible while slithering into the narrow tunnel.

Not being able to hear if I'm making

noise is a major drawback.

The ground was rugged, but whoever dug it, gave it a nice, steady incline leading to the surface.

I wouldn't feel the air getting colder or see a faint light shimmering in the distance if the tunnel was a dead end. She inched farther up, lugging her snowshoes behind her. The light grew brighter. After what felt like an eternity, she emerged from the hole in the shed.

Grateful to have escaped the foul smell of the cellar, she peeked around the doorway, breathing in the fresh scent of winter.

An RCMP officer with short blond hair straddled a snowmobile parked along the side wall.

This isn't the same officer. Confused, she watched him put his helmet on and ride away. *Why would the brown-haired officer hide me from his colleague?*

Suspicious of his motives, she strapped her snowshoes on and fled into the forest.

* * *

To buy himself more time, Landon adjusted and readjusted the straps around the body in his sled. Once he could no longer see or hear Tobin's snowmobile, Landon re-entered the cabin and lifted the trap.

In the semi-darkness, he saw nothing. *Great job hiding in the shadows in silence, Raven.*

Since asking her to come up was pointless, he turned on his flashlight and descended the ladder.

The cellar was empty.

Stumped by her disappearance, Landon shed lights on the walls. A hole appeared behind the ladder. Upon closer inspection, the hole resembled the opening of a tunnel. When Landon sent her down, he never imagined another escape might lie beneath the ground.

That's why Tobin didn't see you. She had to have crawled into the tunnel, but how far she had gone was a mystery his flashlight couldn't illuminate.

Worries overshadowed his frustration at not being able to see her. She could be stuck inside, injured, or unconscious, or she could have resurfaced at the other end, assuming no section of the tunnel had collapsed.

For your sake, Raven, you better be a tunnel rat.

Landon tried squeezing into the opening, but no amount of bending or twisting allowed both his shoulders in. After a few minutes, he gave up and headed outside in search of the exit.

Snowshoe prints led away from a doorless shed in which he discovered a large hole.

* * *

He kissed me. He trapped me underground. And he hid me from his colleague.

Every heavy step that Fate took embedded the officer's actions deeper into her brain, where she couldn't reconcile the three elements. In the cabin, she had believed he had her best interests at heart, never imagining his actions might conceal a more sinister motive.

She couldn't go back to the cave. The stretcher had left too much of a clear path between the cave and the cabin. She would be found in no time.

These men are bound by duty to serve and protect, not take advantage of women like me. Angry and despondent, Fate slogged through the forest away from the cabin, the cave, and Meg's body.

Chapter 10

Eager to resume his search for Raven, Landon entered the RCMP garage at dawn. His snowmobile was parked next to Beck's SUV, but he wasn't alone on the premises.

Surprised to see his sergeant checking the air pressure in his tires this early in the morning, Landon approached him. "Sarge? Is something wrong?"

Beck ventured a glance over his shoulder. "Nothing serious, but I did some digging last evening. The cabin where you found the body belonged to Arnold Thomson and his wife, Margret. Eight years ago, Arnold was stabbed to death in his cabin. Margret was a suspect, but she disappeared before she was apprehended. It's a cold case, and it's all yours, but wouldn't it be poetic justice if Margret came back after all these years only to die where she killed her husband?"

Very poetic indeed. "The woman hasn't been identified yet." Before taking her to the morgue, Landon had followed the snowshoe prints leading away from the shed, but it had started to snow, and he had lost Raven's trail. Nonetheless, he had kept searching for her until darkness forced him to return. "I only dropped her body off last night, so I doubt Caleb had time to process her, but I'll check with him later today."

His sergeant circled his SUV. "After he stumbled onto you at the cabin, Tobin discovered a recently inhabited cave and lots of pelts." Beck squatted next to the left front tire and unscrewed the valve cap. "Since it's possible your dead woman lived there, you may want to check it out."

* * *

She swung the axe above her head and, with a swift blow, hit the log. The wood split, the halves falling in the snow on either side of the stump. She bent to pick up another log.

A snowball flew in front of her eyes. Startled, she looked toward the shed.

A boy slapped his mitts together, grinning. An officer scooped him up and tossed him over his shoulder. Drawn by the child's laughter and the officer's warm brown eyes, she ran toward them.

A gusty storm swept across her path, blinding her. She slipped onto a sheet of ice. It cracked, spurting water in the frigid air. The gap grew wider.

A bloody face rose from its depths,

stealing her breath.

Fate bolted into a sitting position, gasping for air. Rattled by the nightmare lingering at the edge of her consciousness, she stared at the broken window.

Daylight filtered in, diffusing a soft glow inside the only shelter she had stumbled onto after escaping the cellar. The shed where she had abandoned the officer days earlier.

Surprised to still be alive and not cold, she sought to recapture the image of the child. His elusive name burned the tip of her tongue. *The boy is real. I feel the connection between us.*

The brown-haired, brown-eyed officer was more of a mystery. Despite his strange behaviour, her subconscious refused to perceive him as a threat, even though he had locked her in the cellar.

Her stomach rumbled. She tore her gaze from the window and gazed down. A silver survival blanket had bunched down onto her lap. As she pulled it up, the realization that she didn't have a blanket last night struck her. She recoiled against the wall, bewildered, then looked around.

Less than ten feet away, the officer haunting her thoughts sat on the floor, his back against the closed door. Her snowshoes rested on his lap.

Panic rose inside her chest.

"Why on earth didn't you wait for me?" His stationary position and blank expression bared no insight into his mind, but the crisp movement of his lips conveyed his aggravation. "You could have frozen to death overnight."

If he hadn't found her and draped a blanket over her, she might never have woken up. *If he'd meant me harm, he wouldn't have saved me, but he wouldn't have trapped me inside that cellar either.* Panic morphed into frustration at her inability to understand his motives. "You hid me from another officer. Why should I trust you?"

He approached, then kneeled in front of her. "Until I rule out Tobin as a suspect, it's best if he doesn't know you and Eja survived the explosion."

"Explosion? Eja?" The name echoed like a flitting memory. "Who's Eja?"

A look of utter shock overshadowed the officer's rugged features.

* * *

Amnesia explained her behaviour, but Landon still felt dazed, like someone had smacked him over the head. Again. "What's your real name, Fate?"

Quiet defiance burned in her eyes. "You seem to know a lot about me, so why don't you tell me?"

"Your real name is Raven Brook." He

drew her name in the dirt covering the floor, but for fear of distressing her, he refrained from mentioning Eja again at this time. "I've been coming back here every day since I woke up with a huge lump on my skull."

She grimaced in pain. "I'm sorry Meg hit you. She didn't trust the Mounties."

Smart woman. Landon had good reasons not to trust his colleagues, but he would have liked to hear Meg's. "Did Meg have a last name, Raven?"

She shrugged. "Meg never said."

"How did you end up in her company, Raven?" Hoping to give her a sense of identity, Landon used her name as often as possible.

"I woke up in Meg's cave after she saved me from the two men who attacked me where the river splits in two." She rubbed the back of her head, frowning. "I don't remember them, or why I was alone in the forest... I was hit on the head. It's affecting my memory."

Two men attacked you, and one of them—or a third one—blew up your cabin? That's not a coincidence. Landon's first thought was for the trio who killed her grandfather. Unfortunately, neither she nor Meg was in any shape to identify the perpetrators. "Did Meg describe these two men, Raven?"

"Not really, but five years ago, she saw them kill a white elder near the same place. His name may have been Arnie. She was afraid to be arrested and framed for his murder if she reported them. After saving me, she dumped my snowmobile in a pond and staged my death so they would stop chasing me." A flitting shadow darkened her eyes. "How am I supposed to know who to trust if I can't remember who tried to kill me?"

Landon was shocked to learn Meg had witnessed Marshall's death and disappointed she had remained silent.

"If you can't trust me yet, Raven, trust your instincts. I don't know who Arnie is, but the elder's name was Gramp Marcel Marshall." Landon also drew her grandfather's name in the dirt in case seeing it written jogged her memory. "You found him dead in the forest and glimpsed his killers as they fled."

"I was there?" Not an ounce of recognition crossed Raven's face. "Meg said there were three killers. Two men and a teenager, but not the teenager who was framed for his murder. Is the blond officer involved?"

"The blond officer's name is Zane Tobin. Until I figure out who's involved, I'm not willing to trust Tobin, or anyone else for that matter." Pieces of the puzzle were falling into places, but Landon still couldn't see the full picture. "If you hadn't crawled into that tunnel, Tobin would have seen you. That was smart thinking on your part. The day Meg hit me, were you the one who brought me here?"

Raven gave a slight nod of the head. "Meg disagreed, but I couldn't abandon you."

Her actions heartened Landon. "I owe you my life. Can I ask why you chose this shed?"

"According to Meg, your Marcel Marshall lived in these parts. I was looking for his cabin. I was hoping his family would take you in, but this shed was the only shelter I stumbled onto." She gazed at her surroundings. "There was a big, friendly, three-legged German Shepherd hiding inside. The dog acted like it knew you."

"Her name is Rusty. She's a big softy. I took her home with me." Landon held the beautifully crafted snowshoes up with the rabbit paws swinging from the leather straps. "Marshall's snowshoes were piped with rabbit paws, but they went missing from the crime scene. Where did you get these?"

"Meg said the killers threw away Marshall's snowshoes after they beat him. They fled into the forest after they heard an engine. Meg gathered the snowshoes and then followed the killers. She wanted to see what they looked like. Their snowmobiles were parked near a trap, a few kilometres from the river. The two men removed their masks before donning their helmets. That's how she recognized them. The teenager kept his, so she never knew who he was, but he was thinner than the two native teenagers accused of Marshall's murder. There was also a dead lynx strapped to one of their snowmobiles. Meg believed the trap belonged to Marshall and that the killers stole the lynx. When she checked the trap, Meg found blood and a hunting knife in the snow. She wasn't sure who dropped it, but it was sharp, so she kept it along with Marshall's snowshoes. They're beautiful, aren't they?" Raven's face lit up with admiration. "Could you please give the snowshoes back to Marshall's family? They belonged to them."

"They belong in this shed, Raven. Marshall lived here with his granddaughter." Landon was amazed she had found her way home despite her amnesia. "After his death, his granddaughter stayed in his cabin, but someone blew it up last week. I suspect Marshall's killers."

"They blew up his cabin five years after killing him?" She cast a dubious look in his direction. "That makes no sense." The blow that stole her memory hadn't hindered her reasoning skills. "What happened to his granddaughter? Did she die too?"

If Raven's life wasn't in danger, Landon would laugh at the irony that the answer to her questions was locked in her mind. "I have no idea why someone rigged the propane tank and set off an explosion while his granddaughter was on a snowmobile ride in the forest, but I wish she could remember."

"His granddaughter was on a snowmobile ride when..." Her voice trailed off, but Landon could hear the wheels inside her brain connecting the dots. "Marshall was my grandfather?"

* * *

Raven gave the shed a second look, seeking forgotten answers amid the destruction.

Something drew me here. Not once but twice. This was home, and although she couldn't remember, she felt it in her heart.

An image emerged in front of her eyes, an image full of holes and surrounded by thousands of questions.

The brown-haired officer hadn't realized she had developed amnesia until he mentioned the explosion and Eja. Her reaction had triggered a major shift in their conversation. She sensed the name was as significant as the event. "Who's Eja?"

His expression softened. "Eja is an awesome little boy. We were playing in the treehouse outside your cabin when the explosion levelled it."

"You were here with him?" Bewildered by the implications, she grabbed her head in a futile attempt to jog her memory. "Why? Who is he?"

The officer tapped her boot, prompting

her to return her gaze to him. "You're a social worker, Raven. Eja is under your care. You do an amazing job with him, and you're a great listener."

Great listener? Yeah… sure… Once the officer learned she had trouble hearing, his opinion would change for the worse. "At night, I dream of a child. Does Eja have blue eyes?"

"Yes, he does." A tender smile fluttered on the officer's lips. "He's safe, Raven."

It was obvious that the boy held a special place in the officer's heart. "You said you've been coming back here every day. Why?"

"I was hoping you would eventually come home." His gaze enveloped her in a warm embrace. "I promised Eja that I would find you and keep you safe. You'd make my life easier if you'd stop running away from me."

Her instincts pushed her to trust him. "Lucky for you, I've run out of places to hide. Would you tell me more about Eja and the men chasing after me?"

"I will, but first we need to find you a safe place to hide." The officer stood up, and with the snowshoes tucked under his left arm, he offered his right hand. "Would you come with me, Raven Brook?"

Hoping her instincts hadn't steered her wrong in the past, she folded the blanket and took his hand. "I don't know your name."

"Corporal Landon Steele." He gently squeezed her hand. "You call me Landon."

* * *

While Landon waited at the edge of the forest for darkness to cover his final approach to his house, he brought Raven up to speed on the events and people surrounding her life, omitting only two details.

When the time was right, he would tell her about Eja being her son and witnessing Harrison's beating.

"It feels so strange." She straddled the seat of his snowmobile with a half-eaten granola bar in her mitten. "It's like trying to remember a fading dream."

"Would you like to meet your brother Caleb? He could examine your head." The offer presented some challenges, like preventing the doctor from mentioning Eja, securing a meeting place, and trusting a man who couldn't keep a straight face, but Landon was willing to risk it for her health.

"It's a bad idea. The less my brother knows, the safer for everyone. Besides, what would he do? Prescribe a memory pill?"

As much as Landon would like an instant remedy to her condition, he agreed with her assessment. "Once you finish eating, put my helmet on so no one recognizes you. It's almost time to head home."

Amazed to learn the dog belonged to her, Raven snuggled with Rusty on the kitchen floor of Landon's mobile home. "Are you sure I'll be safe hiding here?" It seemed too daring to keep her within footsteps of the detachment. "What if someone comes for a visit?"

"Stay away from the windows and keep the blinds down. Rusty doesn't like strangers. If anyone knocks, she'll bark at them until they walk away." Bent over the oven, Landon scrambled an omelet in a frying pan, but each time he spoke, he looked at her.

The coincidence baffled her. "I promise to be careful."

"Have a seat." He transferred the omelet onto a single plate and placed it on the table. "I'm not what you would call a chef, but I haven't poisoned anyone in a long time."

The aroma wafting across the kitchen tantalized her taste buds. "There's enough for two. Aren't you joining me?"

"I need to see Caleb before he leaves the clinic. I'll eat later."

She sat at the table and took a bite. "This is delicious."

"Glad you like it." Landon nudged Rusty toward two plastic bowls. "Time to eat and let Raven enjoy her meal."

"Rusty trusts you," Raven observed, pleased that her dog's instincts mirrored hers.

"I'm fond of her too." He put his jacket back on. "While I'm gone, make yourself at home. There's more food where that came from and there are towels in the hallway closet. I apologize if the bathtub isn't too clean. Just use the shower. If you need clothes, feel free to rummage through my drawers and borrow whatever fits you."

A comforting familiarity existed between them, and she relished the warm feeling spreading inside her chest. "Thanks, now go. You don't want to miss Caleb."

Once her stomach was contentedly full, Raven tidied the kitchen before opting for a long, cleansing shower.

As she dried herself, light flashed through the bathroom blinds.

What was that about? The road and the driveway were on the other side of the house. There shouldn't be any light reflecting in the bathroom window.

Unsure what to make of it, Raven fingered a slat down and peeked out. A hooded silhouette, flashlight in hand, scurried toward the RCMP garage then peeped through a window, the light briefly reflecting on the glass.

Unsettled by the nearby presence of a prowler, Raven entered Landon's bedroom without touching any electrical switches.

Dim light from the kitchen illuminated her search through his dresser and closet. The clothes she had worn for days on end lay on the bathroom floor, smelly and filthy. Until they went for a spin in the washer on the heavy-duty cycle, there would be no wearing them.

She donned a heavy flannel shirt, tucked it into dark sweatpants, then yanked on the waist cord until the pants stayed above her hips.

I look like a scrawny version of Landon. Amused by the thought, she continued her search in the entrance closet. Rusty stared at her from the kitchen.

The fur coat borrowed from Meg hung next to a dark grey bomber jacket. Raven slipped on her mukluks and donned the bomber jacket. "You stay here, Rusty. I'll be right back."

* * *

Landon entered the morgue. Hunched over the counter like an old man, Caleb wrote in a notebook.

"Hello, Doc."

"Steele?" Caleb closed the notebook and placed the pen on its cover. "I was waiting for you. Any sign of Raven or Eja?"

I'm sorry, Doc, but I can't alleviate your torment yet. "No, but I'm not giving up."

Lying to protect innocent victims had never bothered Landon. Until today. "What can you tell me about the victim?"

"Her prints aren't in the system, but my receptionist Ayita recognized her right away. They went to high school together. Everyone called her Meg, but her full name was Margret Daisy Armstraight. She disappeared after her husband Arnold Thomson was found dead in their cabin." Caleb lowered the sheet covering her face. "According to Ayita, Arnie was a thug who liked gambling, drinking, and beating women. He also owed money to the wrong people. The scar on Meg's cheek is just one of the injuries she suffered at his hands. I ran a body scan. It would be faster to list the few bones that were never broken instead of the ones showing signs of fracture and healing."

So, Arnie was Arnold, and Meg was his punching bag. No wonder she made a good suspect in his death and was afraid to be arrested. "I heard rumours she fled into the forest to avoid prosecution. Do you think she could have killed her husband?"

"Anyone can kill in self-defence, but I'm sure you already know that. I'll dig up Arnie's autopsy report and see what the medical examiner's findings were at the time." Caleb repositioned the white sheet over her head. "As for Meg, she suffered a massive stroke and died. There's nothing suspicious about her death."

"That's good." The last thing Landon

needed was another bloody murder to investigate. Still, he wished he had had a chance to talk to Meg. "This is irrelevant, but I have a buddy back home who was smacked over the head. He was up and running a few days later, but he can't seem to remember anything, not even his children. His wife doesn't know what to do with him. Any suggestions?"

"Head trauma is tricky. Unfortunately, there's not much doctors can do. Time will tell if your friend recovers his memory. All I can suggest is patience and a good psychologist to help him and his family cope with his condition."

* * *

A strong, cold wind whipped Raven's face, giving her hope it also muffled her steps in the snow.

The prowler headed toward the RCMP building. His flashlight illuminated his steady progression around the evergreens growing between the detachment and Landon's home.

Careful to keep her distance, Raven followed between the trees.

The prowler stopped behind the detachment, underneath the spotlight affixed above the back door. He touched what appeared to be a keypad. Seconds later, the door swung open. He entered.

A light flickered inside the detachment, visible through the middle window, then Raven caught a reflection in the window farther left.

Determined to uncover the identity of the intruder, she crouched low and approached the detachment from the opposite end, skimming her way along the exterior wall. Once she reached the last window, she cautiously peeked through the frosty corner.

A lamp was on, illuminating a desk. The intruder hovered near an open drawer, holding some sort of envelope. The hood fell onto his shoulders.

Raven gasped in surprise. *He's a woman?* The female intruder turned off the lamp, but her name whirled in Raven's mind. *I know I know her. Come on, memory.*

Frustrated over her amnesia, Raven moved away from the window.

Someone grabbed her by the shoulders and spun her around, pushing her back to the wall. A scream travelled up her throat and died, muffled by a leather glove covering her mouth. Raven kicked and punched, desperate to fight him off. His body pressed into hers, hindering her breathing. He cupped her face with both hands, forcing her head up.

Their gazes met, and he kissed her.

Landon wrapped her in his arms. *Bear with me, Raven.*

The tension in her body lessened, and she snaked her hands between them, gripping the front of his jacket. He brushed her cheek with his thumb. Her lips quivered, igniting a fire under his skin.

Caught off guard by his own reaction, Landon swallowed hard. *Don't lose your head, Steele.*

The tip of his tongue brushed her lips. They slowly parted, her timid response testing his willpower.

A light shone in his eyes. "Stop right there."

Interrupted by Beck, Landon quickly nudged Raven's head in the crook of his shoulder, concealing most of her face with his glove. "Sarge? I... I didn't hear you."

"I see that." Beck aimed his flashlight at Raven's body, but no sign of recognition lit up his eyes. "Who's the broad?"

"Her name's Fate. She had a little too much to drink. I was taking her home." Landon had no idea how much of their conversation Raven was reading, but he was grateful she was playing along.

"Are you taking me for an idiot, Steele? You're in uniform, and your hands are all over her." His sergeant berated him in a low, raspy voice. "Take her home, right now. I don't want to deal with a complaint of sexual harassment against you. Understood?"

"Yes, Sarge." The woman in his arms tightened her hold on his jacket, prompting Landon to stroke her back to appease her. "We're leaving right now. Good night, Sarge."

* * *

Confused and wary of Landon's indecipherable expression, Raven retreated at the end of the couch.

"I followed your steps in the snow." Landon paced back and forth across the living room, his gaze locked on her. "What the bloody hell were you thinking snooping around the detachment?"

While he shielded her from his sergeant, his glove had only covered one of her eyes. Thanks to the flashlight, she had read his sergeant's lips, but the way her head leaned against his shoulder had prevented her from seeing Landon's responses.

If she asked him about their conversation, he would know something was amiss. The strength with which Landon dragged her into his house had spoken of his anger. Telling him she couldn't hear would only infuriate him further. He would call her irresponsible for venturing outside in the dark with limited senses.

"I wanted to know who the woman was." Raven forced herself to modulate her voice, to keep it low and even. "And stop yelling at me. I was only trying to help."

Landon stilled near the television. "What woman?" His gaze softened. "And for the record, I wasn't yelling."

Her dog jumped on the couch, cuddling against her. Raven sought comfort in the warm, furry body. "The woman whose steps you missed."

His face warped into a quizzical look, and Landon joined her on the couch. "I'm listening."

Under his intense stare, she recounted the entire episode. Not once did Landon interrupt. After she finished, he placed his hand on her forearm but remained quiet.

The prolonged silence unsettled her. "Do you believe me?"

"Sorry, I was thinking." He gently squeezed her arm, and a warm sensation streamed through her body. "Yes, I believe you, except I only saw Beck. He arrived as I caught up with you. I didn't mean to make you uncomfortable, but I needed to protect your identity. Kissing you was the only diversion I could think of at that moment."

In the heat of the encounter, she had enjoyed the kiss. "No need to apologize. You only did your duty." The words left a sour taste in her mouth. She was glad she couldn't hear them.

"Yeah... duty..." He retrieved his hand.

"Only the officers know the code to the back door, and the only female officer currently assigned here is Mathis, but she's on maternity leave. I can't imagine her lurking around when she has a new baby at home. Besides, a new code is generated each week. Are you sure whoever you saw didn't use some sort of electronic device to bypass the code?"

Raven replayed the break-in in her mind. "If she had something in her hand, it would have been small because I didn't see anything. It only took her a second, maybe two, to open the door. Don't those devices take longer to break a code?"

"They usually do." Landon drummed his fingers on his thigh, sporting an enigmatic expression. "Once Beck goes home, I'll take you into my office."

"Me?" Rusty's ears pricked up as if the furry female agreed with Raven that it didn't sound like a good idea. "Why?"

"There are no cameras inside or outside the detachment, don't ask me why, so I need you to recreate every move that woman made. Maybe it'll jog your memory of where you might have seen her before your attack."

Chapter 11

The reconstruction of the intruder's actions had only raised more questions. Seeking answers, Landon drove to the end unit of the townhouse where Tobin lived.

The constable's cruiser was parked in his unplowed driveway. The front porch hadn't been shovelled since the last storm, and no lights were reflected in the windows, but a lamppost illuminated large boot prints leading away from the cruiser.

Landon followed the prints to a back door where he rang the doorbell, again and again, until someone yanked the door open.

"Get lost, Steele." Tobin slammed the door.

Unfazed by the greeting, Landon propped his boot forward, stopping the door from closing. He then took advantage of his colleague's bewilderment to invite himself in. "We need to talk."

Wearing nothing but a pair of blue pajama pants, Tobin backtracked toward the kitchen table. "You have no right to barge in here."

"And you have no right to conceal

documents." Landon pointed at the closest chair. "Have a seat."

The constable squared his shoulders and crossed his arms over his bare chest. "Get out."

As much as Landon abhorred pulling rank, Tobin's lack of cooperation didn't give him much of a choice. "Take a seat, *Constable*," Landon commanded in a slow, cavernous voice. "That's an order."

Tobin sat in the farthest chair, glaring. "I'll have your badge, Steele. You're not going to outrank me for long."

At the rate you're going, Tobin, I wouldn't wage my career on it if I were you. "Let's cut to the chase. Would you like to guess what I found taped underneath your drawer at the detachment?" Underneath the drawer opened by the intruder, Landon had found torn pieces of tape. "I'll give you a hint. It wasn't chewing gum."

The question appeared to deflate Tobin's arrogant demeanour. "You're going to pay for this."

His suspicion heightened, Landon leaned his shoulder against the refrigerator. "How about we settle for an explanation?"

Tobin slumped in his chair. "I found the paternity test while I was cleaning Harrison's desk."

"A paternity test? Do you think I'm that gullible?" Landon stifled his surprise behind feigned indignation. "No one leaves a paternity test lying around in a desk."

"It wasn't exactly in his desk..." The constable's gaze wandered around the kitchen. "More like under his second drawer. What was I supposed to do? Leave it there for the world to find? Alessi didn't need another proof of her husband's betrayal. She's already suffered enough public humiliation."

Landon knew only one Alessi. "How thoughtful of you. Does Harrison's widow know about the test?"

"Yes. Her husband was cheating on her and she was distraught over the possibility that he'd fathered a child with another woman. When she learned he'd taken a paternity test, she begged me to find it and destroy it." Desperation spilled into Tobin's voice. "If you have an ounce of decency left, Steele, you'll burn it and never speak of it again."

"You want *me* to be the decent guy?" The irony amused Landon. "Why didn't *you* destroy it?"

"The damn test was negative. I didn't think it was a big deal. I just wanted to rub Raven's nose in it." Spit flew out of Tobin's mouth. "She had no right to turn me down when she doesn't even know who fathered her bastard."

A wave of anger washed over Landon. He battled the current to repress it. "Who else knows about that paternity test?"

"Aside from you, me, and Alessi? Try anyone else Harrison might have told. I sure would have loved to see the expression on Raven's face when she learned the truth. It's too bad she blew up before I paid her another visit."

Disgusted by his colleague's behaviour, Landon walked out.

* * *

The blue-eyed child ran toward her, his laughter echoing in the crisp autumn morning. She opened her arms, beckoning him into their folds. He reached out... and vanished into thin air.

Raven woke up in bed, tears running down her cheeks.

"Eja..." His name caressed her lips, a sweet plea to her battered brain to remember him.

Sleeping in Landon's pajamas and bed, on his insistence, hadn't brought any restful sleep, only catnaps haunted with memories of the past. The pillow smelled of him, a reminder of the phony kiss they shared.

"This nonsense has to stop." She didn't know the man beneath the uniform. Sane women didn't develop feelings for strangers.

Frustrated, she let her gaze wander around the sparse bedroom.

Landon had been at her cabin the day of the explosion, babysitting Eja and hacking her computer. That didn't seem like the normal behaviour of an officer. Deep down she felt they might be more than acquaintances. "Landon…"

At the sight of the silhouette standing near the door, a current of fear zapped through her body. She glanced around for a weapon. The ceiling light came on, blinding her.

Through flapping eyelids, she recognized him and relaxed. "You frightened me."

"I heard my name. I didn't mean to scare you." He wore his uniform, but his holster was missing, and the first few buttons of his shirt were undone. A few dark hairs escaped through the gap.

"How long have you been back? Did you get to talk to Tobin?" Not being able to hear was a huge inconvenience. "And where's Rusty?" She had last seen her dog curled up at the foot of the dresser.

"Rusty is sleeping underneath the window in the living room." Landon approached the bed. "And yes, I talked to Tobin, but I'm not sure what to make of his revelations."

The intensity with which he scrutinized her sparked a brushfire down her belly. "Why do I have the feeling it wasn't drugs concealed underneath the drawer?"

"It was a paternity test taken by Gage Harrison. He kept it at the office. His widow asked Tobin to steal it and destroy it to protect her reputation." A blank expression concealed Landon's opinion on the matter. "The result was negative, but Tobin kept it with the intent of blackmailing the mother with it."

"He's blackmailing the mother with a negative test?" *How's that supposed to make sense?* "Did he name her? Is she the intruder?"

"He named her, but she is not the intruder." Landon articulated slowly, the lack of contractions adding finality to his statement. "Tobin thinks I'm the one who found the test under his drawer. I didn't tell him about the woman you saw."

"I see..." Raven was tempted to ask why he ruled out Harrison's lover, but she sensed now wasn't the time to satisfy her curiosity. "There are only two women embroiled in that paternity test, Landon, and you already eliminated one. That leaves his widow. Maybe she heard about Tobin's blackmailing scheme and surmised he lied about destroying it." Another plausible motive dawned on Raven. "Or maybe the widow is afraid Tobin lied about the result. What if he never showed her the negative result? What if she only has his words that the test was negative? In her place, I'd be suspicious of Tobin for trying to blackmail a woman with a negative test."

"Tobin thinks I'm in possession of the paternity test, so he can't lie to me about the result, but you may be right about Harrison's widow not trusting him. I'll admit she makes a good suspect. The question I can't answer yet is how the intruder got her hands on the door code, but that's tomorrow's problem." Landon squeezed her forearm, turning her insides into mushy jelly. "Go back to sleep. I'll see you in the morning."

* * *

Raven read the note left on the kitchen table beside a package of multigrain bagels.

> *I took Rusty for a walk*
> *and fed her. She'll be fine until*
> *I get back from work. Landon*

The officer had taken her dog in and out of the house, then left without rousing Raven from her sleep. At this rate, he would soon suspect her hearing loss.

Can't hear and can't remember. Not a great combination. Raven nibbled on a bagel while rummaging through the cupboards. Hiding under his colleagues' noses was a calculated risk, but she had come up with an idea to lower the odds of being recognized.

The cupboard under the sink contained an empty spray bottle. She took it into the bathroom, where she filled it with the hydrogen peroxide she had seen in the medicine cabinet.

182

Her reflection stared back at her from the bathroom mirror. One application wouldn't be enough to transform her into a bleached blonde. At best, it would turn her dark hair into an orangey shade of brown.

Changing her appearance required more drastic measures.

* * *

Landon toured Meg's cave, looking for clues and seeking to erase any traces of Raven's stay.

The half dozen pelts thrown on the floor amid dry branches of evergreens gave no clear indication of how many people slept inside, but the lone pillow with a beige nightgown folded on top suggested only one occupant. A woman.

He looked for any piece of clothing that Raven might have worn the day she disappeared. Among a pile of women's clothes stashed in an alcove, he uncovered a red sports bra with matching panties and a new pair of orange and grey striped wool socks.

Raven wore a red and grey parka. Landon wasn't sure about the socks, but the lingerie set looked like something she might wear. Unwilling to take the risk of leaving any incriminating evidence behind, he pocketed the suspicious garments before continuing his search.

A ladle and two hunting knives sat on top of a rain barrel.

Hoping one of them was the knife that Meg recovered near the trap, Landon seized both. *With any luck, one of them once belonged to one of the killers.*

* * *

Raven shampooed her hair twice, then ended the colouring treatment with a heavy dose of conditioning. Running her fingers through her hair, only to stop short of her shoulders, felt weird.

After drying off, she wiped the foggy mirror.

A stranger with curly cinnamon-brown hair stared back at her.

"That's interesting." She would never have guessed that beneath her long, thick hair were bouncy curls eager to escape. The uneven haircut framed her face, giving her a free and youthful appearance. "I could get used to—"

A shadow swept across the window, momentarily darkening the blinds. Wary of the phenomenon, Raven counted to three before peeping through the slats. A cloudless, blue sky watched over the cold and deserted landscape.

Confident in her disguise, Raven peered

through the other windows. From the one above the kitchen sink, she caught sight of an intruder standing by Landon's Jeep. The driver's side window reflected the intruder's puzzlement.

It's that woman again. Determined to add a name or address to her face, Raven slipped on Landon's winter gear.

* * *

Hoping to learn more about the two knives he seized, Landon entered Fish & Games Outdoor Store.

A seasoned guy with more tattoos on his muscular arms than hair on his head manned the counter. "What can I do for you, Officer?" The name Steve Rogers was embroidered in bronze thread on his green polo shirt above a logo depicting a broom and a curling rock.

"I need your expertise, Steve. I have these two old knives." Landon set them on the counter. After five years, looking for prints other than Meg's had been a waste of powder. "Any chance you could tell me when or where they were purchased?"

"This one is handmade." Steve ran his fingers along the blade of the one with the moose antler handle. "Nice craftmanship, but not much of a resale value. If I were you, I'd keep it. It just needs a good sharpening."

He then examined the one with a bear carved on the handle. "This one is a special edition. I know a guy who'd pay good money for it, enough for you to buy two of my bestsellers to replace it."

Many of the knives advertised behind the locked glass counter ranged in the hundreds of dollars. "Why would he buy my old knife instead of buying a new one from you?"

"Your knife may be old, but it's still in very good condition, and identical to the one that Nash lost in the forest some years ago. It was a birthday gift from his mother weeks before she died. I tried to order him another one, but the vendor didn't make them anymore, and no one had any left in stock." The employee leaned his elbows on the counter. "Don't get me wrong, Nash bought new knives since then, but none ever replaced his special edition. He still talks about his mother's knife every time he comes in."

The Nash character jumped to the top of Landon's suspect list. "Would you happen to have a last name and a contact number for Nash?"

* * *

When Landon entered the name Nash Payne in the database at work, his screen lit up like a Christmas tree.

> *Unpaid speeding tickets. Impaired driving. Bar fights. Disorderly conduct. Drug possession and distribution. Hunting mishap. Unsafe discharge of a weapon. Sexual assault. Solicitation. Death threats…*

Payne's rap sheet listed more misdemeanours and felonies than the criminal code.

"You're thirty-eight years old, Payne. How come none of these offences earned you a lengthy holiday behind bars?"

As Landon read further, a pattern emerged. *Payne commits a crime, pleads guilty to lesser charges, receives credit for time served in custody and a lighter jail sentence, is granted early release for good behaviour, commits a new crime, and the same cycle is repeated over and over.* The convicted felon knew how to manipulate people and the system, and that made him twice as dangerous. *Not the type of guy anyone wants to meet alone in the forest.*

The door of the detachment opened, and Tobin strolled in.

"Hey, Tobin." Landon leaned back in his chair. "Do you know a Nash Payne?"

His colleague slammed his cap on the counter. "If you try to sell the paternity test to Nash, he'll chop you into pieces."

After browsing his criminal record, Landon had no trouble picturing the gruesome fate. "What does Nash have to do with the paternity test?"

"Don't play dumb, Steele. Everyone knows Nash is Alessi's uncle, her mom's much younger brother." Each step Tobin took across the floor left a small puddle of melted snow in its wake, ending at his desk. "If you make the mistake of hurting Alessi, he'll seek revenge, and I won't shed a tear at your funeral."

"Nice to know." *If Uncle Nash was involved in the death of Raven's grandfather, and Harrison found out, it might have put him at odds with his wife's family.* The possible ramifications extended far beyond Landon's wildest theories. "I'm going shopping. Make sure you mop the floor during your coffee break."

* * *

Eager to share her discovery with Landon, Raven marched in the snowmobile tracks crisscrossing the open field adjacent to his house.

His RCMP truck pulled into his driveway. Landon stepped out with a big shopping bag, climbed the porch in a few bouncy strides, and entered.

A few minutes later, he returned outside without his cap. His eyes shielded with one hand, he seemingly scanned the surrounding landscape. When he turned toward her, she waved.

The scowl on his face dumped a bucket of snow on her otherwise fruitful day. Raven slowed her approach.

"Lady, I don't know who you are, but—" His eyes widened in shock. "Fate? Is it you?"

Relief washed over her. He had mistaken her for a stranger, only recognizing her when she neared his truck, and used her nickname, which could mean he wasn't a hundred per cent sure of her identity. "It doesn't look like me, does it?"

Landon grabbed her by the shoulders. "You're supposed to be hiding." His hands trembled through the insulation of the bomber jacket. "You're—" A look of panic flitted across his face. "You're going to be the death of me."

"Why?" No one had come within thirty feet of her. She had been careful to remain as inconspicuous as possible. "No one paid any attention to me."

"Trust me." Leaning forward, he brushed a tender kiss on her lips. "Now get in and stay there." Without further explanation, he nudged her inside the house and closed the door behind her.

Mystified by the man responsible for the tingling on her lips, she curled the blind up to spy on him. At the sight of his sergeant marching toward the house, understanding dawned on her.

Swell. Another phony kiss. Miffed by Landon's scheme, she moved away from the window. *Whatever story he intended to concoct had better be good or—*

She tripped over a bag and tumbled on the kitchen floor, sore and undignified. Rusty stared at her from underneath the table with her ears laid back and a sad puppy face. "Yeah, my feelings exactly."

Less than impressed, she picked up the bag responsible for her mishap. It resembled the shopping bag that Landon had carried in. *Who leaves a bag on the floor in the middle of a kitchen?*

Mad at him for his lack of consideration, she emptied the contents onto the floor. She couldn't care less about infringing on the privacy of a man who kissed her for fun.

Sweatpants. T-shirts. Sweatshirts. Boxers. Socks. Toothbrush. Antiperspirant. A hairbrush...

Landon's hair was so short, he didn't need a brush, he didn't even need a comb, but she sure could use one. Another possibility entered her mind, prompting her to take a closer look at his purchases. All the clothes were of neutral colour. Navy blue, grey, black, and forest green. Nothing that stood out in a crowd. And they were all the same size. *Small.*

Two black socks with large feet in them appeared in her corner vision. She twisted around and met Landon's gaze.

"I would have liked to buy you women's clothes, but it would have raised too much suspicion."

The qualms that she harboured toward him sailed away. "That was nice of you. I promise to repay you."

"Don't worry about money." He presented her with a pair of underwear and socks. "I found these in Meg's cave. I'm guessing they're yours?"

Despite the lack of running water, Meg insisted on washing their underwear daily. On the day she died, Raven had worn some of the older woman's garments.

"Yes." Raven stood and sized the officer up. "How did you know?"

An enigmatic smile skirted over his mouth. "It was an educated guess. Your parka, which you may not remember, was red and grey."

Some sort of relationship does exist between us. She felt it even though the exact nature of it still escaped her. "And the socks? They're orange. I'm sure they don't match anything I own."

"They match the new highlights in your hair." He twirled a curly lock between his fingers. "You scare the hell out of me. You cannot just walk out without telling me. You need to think about your... about your safety."

Her heart, the only sound she could hear, beat furiously in her chest. Her gaze was focused on his lips, but when he hesitated, she dared look deeper into his eyes. Something akin to fear, not anger, swirled in their mist. "My safety? Is it all you care about?"

"No..." He caressed her cheeks with the back of his fingers. "I care about you, more than I should under the circumstances."

His touch scrambled her memory, evoking fond images of him and the blue-eyed boy stacking wood near a fireplace. "Your sergeant wasn't too happy he caught you kissing me last night. How did he react this time?"

"He saw you crossing the field and recognized your bomber jacket from yesterday. He wanted to know what you were doing near my house." Landon lowered his hand, leaving behind a feathery caress on her arm. "I told him you were babysitting Raven's dog while I work."

The irony wasn't lost on her. "And he believed you?"

"He urged me to hire someone less likely to cause trouble, so who knows." Another smile touched his lips. "You did a great job changing your appearance. It was a brilliant idea, but you still took an awful risk venturing outside. Please, tell me it was worth it."

"The woman who stole the paternity test, she snooped around again, so I followed her." Proud of her accomplishment, Raven didn't conceal her excitement. "Before you say anything, she didn't look my way once. She walked everywhere, like she had no care in the world."

Landon crossed his arms over his chest. "Keep going."

"She stepped into a few stores, didn't buy anything, but then she met a tough-looking middle-aged guy for lunch at Tim Hortons. He had lots of facial scars." Something in the guy's demeanour had sent shivers down Raven's spine. "They had a heated conversation in the parking lot. Something about a knife."

"A knife?" A small vein pulsed underneath Landon's left eye. "Could you make out other details of the conversation?"

"No, but the woman was furious." Had the guy not jerked his head back and forth, Raven might have figured out what was so special about that knife. As skilled as she seemed to be in interpreting people's words, she couldn't read lips if she didn't see a mouth. "They parted a few minutes later. She walked away on foot. He left at the wheel of a red truck."

Landon retrieved a notepad from his shirt pocket and scribbled something on it. "If you were to see that man again, would you recognize him?"

"He was rather unforgettable." The type of face no woman wanted to meet in a dark alley at night.

"Good." Landon looked pleased. "Did you see where the woman went?"

"She entered the library and came out a few minutes later with a young child. They left in a silver Lexus, licence plate Hotel, Oscar, Tango, Two, Four, One."

"Alessi Harrison has a young daughter and drives a silver Lexus." He pulled two knives from the pocket of his jacket. "These knives were on a barrel in Meg's cave. Could one of them be the one she found near the trap the day your grandfather was killed?"

"Probably... maybe... She did say she kept it, but these are the only knives I saw in the cave." Suddenly, the conversation Raven eavesdropped earlier took on a different meaning. "They couldn't have been arguing about Meg's knife, could they? How could they have known about it?"

"I may have tipped someone off when I showed the knives to Steve." Landon shook his head. "It's a long story."

"I like long stories. So, who's Steve? And don't think about leaving out any details. I don't need more holes in my cheesy memory."

* * *

After lecturing her about the risks of venturing outside, Landon understood Raven's reluctance to enter the detachment a second time around.

She sat at the edge of his chair, her back

straight, ready to bolt. "I feel like a sitting duck."

A feisty and beautiful duck. "Beck and Tobin just left. We have plenty of time. Now I'd like you to pay attention to the screen." He accessed the DMV database. The Lexus registration certificate appeared on the screen alongside the owner's driver's licence. Alessi Harrison.

"That's her. She's the intruder. I guess it's true what they say about never being served better than by yourself, but why is Alessi still snooping around now that she found the paternity test?" Raven's gaze wondered somewhere above his head. "If Meg's knife used to belong to Alessi's uncle Nash, it could implicate him in Gramp's murder. He'll want it back. Your Steve guy at the outdoor store may have given him a call, and Nash may have sent Alessi to look for it. Could Uncle Nash have been the shady guy she argued with?"

In normal times, Landon wouldn't share the details of his investigation with civilians, but he couldn't trust anyone else. Besides, Raven made a great partner. He loved how her mysterious mind worked.

"Hold on." He entered Nash Payne's name in the DMV database. A truck registration certificate appeared alongside his driver's licence.

"It's him, Landon." The gentle hand she pressed on his forearm caught more than his attention, it awoke a longing in his heart.

"And he owns a red truck. Have you ever dealt with him in the past?"

"Not directly, but he possesses a long criminal record." The camera had captured the coldness in Nash's sunken eyes and the harsh scars jarring his face. "I'll be in the archive room for a few minutes." Landon cleared his search and logged out. "Just wait for me here."

As he drew away, his winter jacket caught the handle of his drawer, pulling it open. He elbowed the drawer and then hurried down the corridor.

The online version of Nash's criminal record listed his arrests and convictions, but Landon wanted to look at the original arrest reports in case the arresting officers had scribbled comments that were omitted in the online version.

He browsed through the filing cabinet. *Bloody hell, what happened to the alphabet?* Over the years, a dozen or so individuals with the last name Payne had been arrested, but their police reports weren't filed according to their first names.

Annoyed by the lack of organization, Landon flipped through the Paynes. *Gabriel. Evans. Paul. Bradley. Joseph. Nash—*

I can't believe you're here, Nash, and nobody deleted you.

Landon leafed through the pages. Many officers were convinced Nash didn't act alone when he committed a crime, but every time he pleaded guilty, he also took full responsibility, denying anyone else was involved in his crimes.

How noble of you to protect your accomplice, Nash. Disappointed, Landon refiled the report and rejoined Raven.

"So?" She waited all zipped up. "Did you find what you were looking for?"

"No." His drawer was ajar again. As he closed it, the front door handle rattled. "Someone's coming."

He took Raven's hand and led her toward the back door.

Chapter 12

Relieved to have escaped the detachment without being caught, Raven waited in the vestibule for Landon to shed his winter gear and enter the kitchen before taking her boots off.

The letter she stole from his desk was tucked in her jacket, and she didn't want him to see it.

He grabbed his radio. "What do you want, Tobin?" His face darkened. "I'll be right there." Landon pressed a hand on her shoulder. "An idiot started a brawl at The Bent Elbow. I'll be back as soon as I can. Be careful and no heroics."

Once the RCMP truck was no longer parked in the driveway, Raven sat on the couch with Rusty. Without bothering to remove her coat, she read the letter.

"Don't stare at me like that, Rusty. The letter was in plain view and my name was written on top. I couldn't just leave it in Landon's drawer."

Hoping for answers to the many questions surrounding her past, Raven read it in silence.

Raven Brook was born in Toronto. Mother was a prostitute who died of an overdose when Raven was seven. Father is unknown, probably a john.

After her mother's death, Brook was raised by a fellow prostitute who also had a son, Caleb Marshall. A year later, Grandfather Marcel Marshall took custody of both children. The fate of Caleb's mother is unknown, but prostitutes were the only female role models in Brook's life.

Brook worked as a social worker in Halifax by day, but rumours had it she roamed the streets at night, following in her mother's footsteps. An officer at the Halifax Regional Police recalls arresting Brook in a cheap motel on suspicion of enticing young girls into prostitution, but no charges were ever filed.

"Enticing young girls?" Stunned, Raven reread the paragraph. "My job is to protect children, not victimize them. Child Welfare Services would never have hired me if there had been even a smidgen of truth in those allegations." Besides, the police would have filed charges and opened an investigation if the arrest had held any merits. "Just because my mother and Caleb's were prostitutes doesn't make me one."

Baffled by her alleged presence in a cheap motel, Raven continued.

> *Brook quit a well-paid job in Halifax and moved to Sprucetown. A week later, her grandfather is murdered in the forest. She found his body and implicated three individuals in his death. Her false statement was thrown out after two teenagers confessed to the crime in a suicide note.*
>
> *Harrison couldn't prove she lied to protect the indigenous teenagers. Therefore, she wasn't charged with obstruction of justice.*

"I didn't lie. And Landon believes me." Feeling vindicated, Raven patted Rusty's head. Her dog jumped off the couch and disappeared into the kitchen.

Unfazed by her sudden departure, Raven kept reading.

> *Nine months later, she gave birth to a son, Eja, but*

Aghast, Raven stared at the words unraveling her past. "Eja is my son?"

The letter slipped from her fingers and glided on the floor, stopping against a black leather boot.

"How dare you lie to me?" She lifted her chin, lashing at Landon. "You better—"

A smirk disfigured the face of the blond officer. "Raven? It's a pity you're still alive."

Startled by Tobin's sudden appearance, she leaped to her feet. "Landon will be back any moment. If I were you, I'd leave now."

"Steele is busy rounding up the drunken patrons I riled up, and I locked your beast in the bathroom." The constable rested his hand on his holster. "You're lucky I didn't shoot him for ripping my pants."

Rusty was a her, not a him. For reasons Raven couldn't fathom, Tobin's ignorance irked her. "What do you want?"

"I want the envelope that Steele stole from my desk, the one with..." He glanced at the letter, then stamped it with his boot. "The one with the paternity test in it. I won't let Steele consort with you to bring shame on Alessi."

"Shame?" Raven questioned the accuracy of her lip reading, but regardless of what she might have misunderstood, she had the uncanny feeling that Tobin wouldn't appreciate learning the widow masqueraded as a burglar. "If you'd destroyed the test when you had a chance, you wouldn't be in that predicament."

The officer took a threatening step forward. "Where's your boy?"

Images of her son juxtaposed with memories of her encounter with Landon in the shed. His expression had softened when he told her that Eja was safe.

At the time, his words had held little significance. Tonight, they meant everything. She would be damned if she let anyone touch her son. "Eja is gone."

"In this case, he won't miss you." Tobin drew his gun. "Give me the paternity test."

"I don't know where it is." Suspicious of his obsession, she inched toward the fireplace. Meg's hunting knives were on the mantle, the closest one an arm's length away. "Why don't you ask Landon?"

"This isn't a game." The officer lurched at her.

She spun around, raising her fist. A jarring blow to her side sent her crashing to the floor. Tobin jammed her arm behind her back, and in an agonizing twist, pulled her up to her feet.

Tears of pain and anger pooled in her eyes. "Let me go."

His gloved hand cupped her chin, forcing her to look at him. "I'm tired of being rejected, Raven. You slept with Harrison under his wife's nose and tried to pin your son on him. When that backfired, you seduced Steele. You're nothing but a piece of trash ready for..."

As the implication sank in, Raven lost focus on his lips. *This can't be true. Whoever Raven Brook may have been, I'm not that Raven. Not anymore. I would never do the things she's accused of doing.* "No!"

Assailed by conflicting emotions, she thrust her knee forward, connecting with his inflated manhood. His fingers pressed into her cheeks. He shoved her toward the fireplace. She tripped over the tool set and kicked a bucket. Ashes rose into the air, filling her nostrils. She tumbled on the floor, spitting and coughing. Tobin gripped her hand and squeezed. Something snapped, and serrated pain seared through her fingers.

Her vision blurred. She blacked out.

* * *

Landon reined in his growing frustration and drove home.

The brawl had erupted shortly after Tobin was seen leaving The Bent Elbow, but the identity of the instigators remained a mystery. Nobody knew anything, heard anything, or did anything, not even the owner-bartender who faced costly damages.

Most of the patrons deserved to spend the night sobering up in a cell, but since

Landon had no interest in babysitting them or cleaning up their mess in the morning, he didn't make any arrests.

Lights filtered through the covered windows of his home. He walked in, eager to see Raven, then froze into the kitchen.

The cupboards and drawers were open, their contents tossed on the counter and the floor. He drew his gun before moving to the other rooms.

In the living room, the ash bucket was pushed in a corner, upside down. The tong, poker, brush, shovel, and tool stand were tipped into a pool of ashes, along with one of Meg's knives and a sheet of paper with a partial boot print on it. He picked it up.

Bloody hell. The information that Tobin had gleaned on Raven belonged in his desk, not on his floor. If Raven read she had a son, she would never forgive him for the omission or trust him again. However, Landon couldn't picture her trashing his home in retaliation.

He holstered his gun, tore the sheet of paper, and tossed the pieces into the fireplace. The knife with the carved bear rested on the mantle.

Whoever ransacked the house wasn't looking for the knife. It left only one other document worth breaking in and searching for in his house. *Harrison's evidence.*

Landon rushed into his bedroom, which had also been ransacked. Bracing himself for the disappearance of his evidence, he removed the loosened baseboard in the closet and slipped a hand underneath the shaggy carpet. The tip of his fingers brushed a corner of the envelope. He heaved a sigh of relief. The evidence was safe, but it didn't explain Raven's disappearance.

Strange whimpers reached his ears.

He pressed the baseboard back in place before following the faint sound to the bathroom.

Something scratched at the door.

"Rusty? Is that you?" The moaning stopped, replaced by barking. "Hold on, girl." Careful not to injure the dog, Landon opened the door slowly. As soon as the gap grew wide enough, Rusty squeezed through and nuzzled him. "I'm glad to see you too, girl." He scratched her behind the ears while scanning the bathroom. The shower curtain was bunched up at one end, and the tub was empty. "Were you alone during the break-in? Did Raven lock you in for your protection? Or did she flee without you?"

Raven was resourceful, that much Landon could attest to, but worries still feasted on him. The German Shepherd dashed out of the bathroom, barking.

Hope of Raven's return surged in Landon's chest. He rounded the corner of the hallway.

Agonizing moans welcomed him in the kitchen.

A cold, wet cloth wiping her face roused Raven's senses, unleashing the details of her recent attack.

Her eyes flew open, and she shrieked in agony.

"Your finger is broken. If I were you, I wouldn't move my hand." Tobin's concern for her well-being riled her up.

"Get away from me." She kicked him. Another agonizing shot ripped through her hand, overshadowing the realization that she wore her boots on the wrong feet.

He dropped the facecloth on her lap dodging her boot. "Do you know where women like you end up?"

No, and I don't care. No woman deserved to be handcuffed to a water pipe under a sink with her back against a toilet bowl. *That's disgusting.* "Where am I?"

"In a quiet place." His overconfidence suggested the bathroom was familiar territory. "Steele is going to worry sick about you. By morning, he'll be ready to trade the paternity test for you. He's such a pathetic loser."

The only loser was the one who broke her finger and showed little respect for the law. "That's kidnapping and extortion. You won't get away with this."

"In his official report, Steele declared you and your boy missing. Once the sergeant learns Steele disguised you and kept you in his home for his personal pleasure, he'll destroy Steele's career. Steele has no choice but to buy my silence." A predatory glint shone in his eyes. "And so do you."

She pulled on the handcuffs, recoiling farther between the toilet and the sink, and muffled another shriek. Her injured finger couldn't bear the slightest motion. "Touch me, and I'll kill you."

"I never forced myself on a woman, and I'm not about to start with you." Tobin ran a hand along her leg. "If you care for Steele, you'll make the right choice."

Raving mad, she slapped his wandering hand. "Over my dead body."

"Hookers like you turn up dead in dumpsters every day. You—" His lips stopped moving. He removed his hand and picked up his phone. "We're not done."

Tobin turned his back to answer but didn't leave the room.

He doesn't care if I listen. This can't be a good sign for me. She caught his reflection in the full-length mirror beside the shower stall. Words flew from his mouth, and to her amazement, she could read his image.

"Of course I want to see you." An air of satisfaction enveloped him. "I'm free all night, Alessi luv."

Alessi Love? Raven stared at the mirror, trying to recapture the sounds she was able to hear and match them to the reversed movement of his lips. *Like in Alessi*

Harrison?

Tobin crouched by her side. "I have a date, but I'll be back by morning. You're lucky the neighbours are gone, or else I'd gag you. Feel free to scream."

A rush of adrenaline raced through Raven's body, and the tip of her good fingers pulsed in anticipation of his departure. "Go to hell."

He stood back, smirking. "I'll tame you, Raven. One way or another."

The threat resonated in her head long after he slammed the bathroom door shut.

I could be in a worse predicament. He could have turned the lights off. In the dark, she would have struggled removing the elbow drainpipe.

Anyone with basic plumbing knowledge would never cuff a prisoner under a sink. *Lucky for me, you're not a handyman, Tobin.*

The ABS pipes were covered with a thin layer of dust. She clasped the slip nut with her stronger hand, which thankfully wasn't the one with a broken digit. Clenching her teeth, she twisted it. *Come on.*

Using her body as leverage, she toiled to loosen the nut. Sweat pooled between her shoulder blades, heat flushed her face, and pain radiated from her hand. *I can do this. I need to do this.*

Back in Landon's house, she didn't remove her bomber jacket, but she recalled taking her boots off. Tobin was probably the one who had put them back on her feet before dragging her outside. While she was grateful for them, she wished for one less layer on her back.

Come on. Twist. It's hot in here. The nut shifted by a few degrees, the small gain energizing her endeavour. *We're getting there.* The nut gave way suddenly.

Brownish slime dripped from the pipe.

Disgusted by the goo coating her hand, she hassled to unscrew the pipe. "You're right, Tobin. We are *not* done."

* * *

Caught off guard by the felon pointing a rifle in his direction, Landon stopped dead in the kitchen doorway. "Payne."

The felon crushed Rusty's head with his work boot, immobilizing the bleeding dog down on the floor. "Hands up!"

Landon slowly raised his hands. As good as a marksman as he was, he couldn't draw his gun faster than Payne could pull the trigger. "Release the dog, Payne. Don't add animal cruelty to your rap sheet."

Payne smirked. "Give me back my knife, and I'll let Brook's flea carpet live long enough to eat one last meal."

The coldness in the felon's voice reflected an emotional void. Once Payne retrieved the knife, anyone else would become expendable.

"I keep it in my office," Landon lied to buy himself some precious seconds. From the corner of his eye, he caught movement on his left. He instinctively lowered his arms but was too slow to react. The blow hit him in the chest, knocking the wind out of him.

* * *

The wind slapped her face, and the snow stuck to her hair. Raven had no idea how long Tobin kept her in captivity, or how long it took her to escape, but Mother Nature had taken advantage of her ordeal to brew up a snowstorm.

Raven raised the collar of the bomber jacket to cover her ears before carefully digging her bare hands back into the pockets. *The cold may be good for the swelling, but I'd rather have a pair of gloves and a hat.*

The gusting wind and heavy snow decreased visibility in the sleepy neighbourhood.

She plodded along unplowed sidewalks, following directions imprinted in her mind. The name of the streets escaped her, but the lampposts dotting the quiet streets with faint circles of light led the way to her brother's clinic.

A green Hummer parked by the side

door beckoned her to enter and go down a flight of stairs. Halfway down, a crack appeared on the wall. It ran up, reaching the light fixture at the junction of the ceiling. *I've been here. Often.*

Heartened by the unequivocal recollection, Raven followed the dim hallway to a large room where a white man with a bouncy red ponytail sterilized medical instruments.

Staring at the man didn't fire up any memories. When Landon told her about her life, she should have asked for a description of her brother. "Caleb?"

His dark gaze grazed over her. "It's the middle of the night. What can I do for—" The muscles in his face seized up. He dropped a long metallic probe into the sink, splashing water on his green scrub. "Raven? Is that you?"

The speed with which he closed the gap between them and the huge hug he gave her warmed her inside, but trapped her injured hand between them. She winced in pain. "My finger is broken."

"Let me see." He forced her to sit on a stool, then pulled her sleeve up, exposing the handcuff and a chafing rash where it rubbed around her wrist.

Raven's animosity toward Tobin morphed into full hatred. "This isn't what you think."

"Really?" Her brother's stare pinned her to the seat. "An explosion obliterated your cabin. You and Eja disappeared. Steele has been looking for you, day and night. I don't think he slept. I sure didn't. I was beside myself, Raven. I feared the worst. Now you're in my morgue at three in the morning with handcuffs dangling from your arm looking like a stranger. What's going on? Where's Eja?"

Learning that Landon had relentlessly searched for her was a soothing balm to her injuries, even if she was still angry with him for not telling her the truth about Eja. "Landon is keeping Eja safe."

"Steele knows you're alive?" A weight seemed to lift from Caleb's shoulders. "Is he the one who cuffed you?"

The thought brought a weary smile to her face. With her propensity to disappear, Landon might soon consider tying her up. "No, it's... it's complicated." She didn't want to implicate Tobin until she talked to Landon. "Landon thinks Gramp's murder and Gage's death are related, that I can identify the killers. That's why they blew up the cabin. They're trying to kill me, to silence me, but I don't know who they are."

The horror of it all was reflected on Caleb's face. "You should be in protective custody." He carefully manipulated her hand. "Not wandering alone at this ungodly time."

And you should be in bed with Annette, not working. The name had popped in her mind, uncensored. Raven sighed. Of all the details trapped in her brain, her memory had chosen to release the identity of Caleb's vain and computer-obsessed girlfriend.

"I'm hiding at Landon's—" A painful jolt travelled from her fingernail to her elbow. "That hurts."

"Sure it does. It's broken." An apologetic smile wrinkled the corners of her brother's eyes. "It feels like a simple fracture, but I need an X-ray to confirm."

"No time for X-rays." She had to get back to Landon before Tobin messed things up. "Can you quickly fix my finger and give me a ride to Landon's house? Please?"

* * *

Raven recognized the blue house with the double garage at the opposite end of Landon's street. From there, it was a five-minute walk to his house, but without Caleb's help, she wouldn't have found her way back.

"Stop here." For everyone's safety, her brother couldn't be seen dropping her off any closer. "I'll walk the rest of the way."

Caleb parked alongside the blue house and then turned toward her. In the dark, she couldn't read his lips, but she took comfort in his touch when he squeezed her forearm.

"Thank you, Caleb. And remember, no one can know we're alive until Landon arrests the killers." She left the warmth of the Hummer, wearing Caleb's big gloves and scarf, and waited on the sidewalk for him to depart.

Instead, he stepped out.

"When I said I'll walk, I meant I, Caleb, not we."

Despite her objections, he nudged her toward Landon's house.

Surrounded mainly by vacant lots, the street was bordered on one side by snowbanks and on the other by the unplowed sidewalk they trudged on.

She stopped in front of a vacant lot where a large spruce grew. Across the street, Landon's side door opened, and light filtered outside.

Two snowmobiles were parked in front of his RCMP truck. Suspicious of the vehicles, Raven pulled on her brother's sleeve, forcing him to crouch alongside her in the shadow of the evergreen.

Two strangers dressed in black snowsuits carried a motionless person into the driveway. The motion-activated lantern above the side door cast a sudden and strong beam of light over them.

Her brother draped a protective arm across her shoulders.

The stranger at the front sidestepped Landon's truck then paused to retrieve something. The one at the back dropped the victim's legs. In the light, a golden stripe swooped down.

Raven's knees buckled. There was no mistaking the RCMP pants. *Landon?* Down on her knees, she stared, helpless. The wind prickled her eyes. She blinked away the moisture building behind her eyelids.

The strangers dragged the officer she believed to be Landon to the closest snowmobile, strapped him to the seat, then each man straddled a ride. The headlights of their snowmobiles came to life within seconds of each other. Vibrations reached her ears. Snow rose in the air, mixing with the storm. They disappeared into the night.

"No!" She dashed across the street and into the house, her brother on her heels. In her haste, Raven missed dodging the sticky blood puddles on the floor. Her stomach revved up. With great effort, she willed its contents to stay down.

Bloody paw prints led her into Landon's bedroom. Curled in front of the dresser, Rusty stared with sad brown eyes. Blood matted the fur around her muzzle.

"What happened, girl?" Raven knelt by her side and stroked her back. "Who did that to you?"

Her brother nudged her out of the way. "I'll take care of Rusty. You look for Landon."

The officer who protected her needed help. Landon hadn't trusted any of his colleagues. Reporting him missing wasn't an option, not with a raging storm quickly erasing the tracks left behind by the abductors.

They took an awful risk kidnapping him within eyeshot of the detachment. The knife with the moose antler handle lay on the floor. Raven borrowed it and then searched for the fob of his RCMP snowmobile.

Out of the blue, the schematic of how to hotwire a snowmobile flashed in her mind. *How come I know that?* Both alarmed and fascinated by her own expertise, Raven nevertheless pushed the thought aside. As skilled as she might be, she couldn't wire snowmobiles equipped with safety systems, and she bet police vehicles entered that category.

The kitchen had been trashed. Among the broken jars on the counter, a fob lay under a transparent shard. *You better be the right one.*

Raven rushed outside and stepped onto something hard.

This is where the abductor bent down, and I saw the golden stripe. Thinking he might have dropped something but not recovered it, she dug the snow out of her print, uncovering a dark wallet.

She flipped it open and expelled a shaky breath. Landon's badge.

* * *

Bounced around like a puppet, with only a rope tied around his chest to keep him from being thrown in the snow, Landon pried his eyes open. The cold burned his face, the bumps tortured his buttocks, and the bindings squeezing his wrists trapped his arms between his back and the backrest of the snowmobile.

Payne's accomplice had struck him, then one of them had taken him for a ride in the forest. The only way these two could avoid being charged for assault and kidnapping was to make sure his body never resurfaced.

The similarity between his predicament and Harrison's fate didn't escape Landon.

The rider swerved left. The rope cut through Landon's jacket, and his right boot slid off the running board, brushing the snow.

No one bothered tying my legs. While it might have been an oversight on their part, it was also possible they never anticipated he would regain consciousness. In his current situation, the element of surprise was about the only thing playing in Landon's favour.

He carefully reeled his leg in without touching the driver. The single headlight pierced through the night. In the distance, a cabin emerged. Landon recognized the red roof.

Of all the places to ditch a body, the tunnel running underneath made the perfect tomb. No one would ever think of looking for him there.

The snowmobile came to an abrupt halt by the shed. His abductor removed his helmet and rose.

Landon brought his knees to his chest and kicked his abductor in the lower back, propelling him into the windshield. It shattered on impact. The guy slumped on the hood, motionless.

A light shone from behind, and the engine of a second snowmobile grew louder.

Bloody hell. Dying wasn't mentioned in the fine print when Landon accepted the assignment.

A knot in the rope pressed against his spine. He wriggled and wiggled, rolling the rope from his chest down to his belly, and bringing the knot closer to his hands. *Come on.*

Steps crunched in the snow.

"Don't move or I'll shoot." The male voice, muffled by the helmet, didn't belong to Payne.

Landon strengthened his back. The accomplice pointed a gun at his chest, a gun sharing an uncanny resemblance with Landon's service weapon. With his best poker face in place, Landon stared into the black visor while playing with the knot. "You and Sleeping Beauty Payne on the hood murdered Gage Harrison, Marcel Marshall, and two teenage boys. If I die, the evidence will go directly to a special investigator in St. John's."

"You have no proof." The accomplice had called his bluff without denying the allegations.

That sounds like a bloody admission of guilt. However, being right about them didn't improve Landon's precarious situation. "Are you willing to bet your freedom on it? And spend the rest of your life in jail for killing a police officer?"

The knot broke loose. Landon lunged at the accomplice and grabbed the hand wielding the gun. The accomplice yanked his arm back, propelling them both into the snow. Landon clung to his opponent's wrist. They tumbled wrestling for the weapon.

A gunshot resonated in the night as scorching pain shot through Landon's back.

Chapter 13

Hidden from view at the edge of the clearing, Raven watched the fight taking place beside the abandoned cabin.

Landon had become entangled with his abductor, and she could no longer differentiate them.

The headlight of one snowmobile cast a white light on the cabin and the clearing while the other snowmobile, the one with the motionless abductor leaning—

Raven muffled a scream.

The abductor, who had moments ago rested over the windshield, joined the fight. Two of them toppled over in the snow, and a third grabbed one of them by his legs.

At the sight of the golden stripe being held up and dragged inside the cabin, Raven's heart sank. *This can't be happening.* She trudged toward the scene, knee-deep in snow.

The one lying in the snow stirred.

She hid behind a snowdrift, then hoping enough snow had accumulated on her hat to turn it white, she ventured a peek.

The one in the snow struggled to stand

up. His accomplice rushed out of the cabin and helped him onto a snowmobile. They rode away together.

When Raven could no longer see them, she pulled a flashlight from her pocket and approached the cabin.

The windshield of the remaining snowmobile was smashed and smeared with blood. More blood tainted the matted snow where Landon had fought and lost his battle.

On a patch of untainted snow, she spotted a gun. She grabbed the weapon and hurried inside.

The man she came to rescue lay sideways on the floor with a reddish stain seeping through the back of his jacket.

She pocketed the gun and slipped off her glove kneeling beside him. "Landon? Can you hear me?" She pressed two fingers against his neck.

The erratic beating of her heart amplified the steady pulse coursing through the tips of her fingers. Relief washed over her, loosening the knot in her stomach. "If you can hear me, don't move. I'll check your injury."

The blood around the edge of the wound had already started coagulating or freezing. "Looks like you were stabbed, not shot." *Though I'm not sure which one is better.* She stuffed her scarf underneath his shirt. "Don't move, I'll get your snowmobile."

She raced to the large trees where she had concealed his snowmobile, remembering the day she disobeyed Meg's orders and drove him to safety. Except this time, he suffered more than just a blow to the head.

The wind unleashing its fury on the forest had draped a layer of snow over the vehicle. She brushed the snow off the seat and then rode into the cabin, stopping alongside his body.

The headlights illuminated the interior of the ramshackle cabin.

Landon stirred.

Pleased to see him regain consciousness, she squatted near him. "Landon?" She caressed his swollen cheek marred with cuts and bruises, relishing for a moment the cold, bristly texture against her bare hand.

His eyelids flickered. "Eja..."

The name of her son caressed his lips. "Where's Eja?"

"My father... Patrick Steele... Cape Breton..." He grabbed her hand. "Safe. Go."

"Right now, Eja is safer with your father than with me." Once this nightmare was over, she would find her son, preferably with Landon's help. If not, she trusted the officer had taken precautionary measures. "I'm not going anywhere without you."

He grimaced in obvious pain. "Raven..."

"Do not Raven me, Steele." Leaving him here alone at the mercy of these killers wasn't an option. "We have to leave before your friends come back, and for the record, you need to stop hanging out with the wrong crowd."

He coughed up a faint smile. "You'll be the death of me... No hospital... Promise."

A sigh built inside her chest. Under different circumstances, she might enjoy being the death of him. Just not tonight. "Fine. No hospital. Now help me get you in the sled."

* * *

The cold helped Landon to stay conscious, but every bump in the snow exacerbated the searing pain in his back.

The deafening detonation still rang in his ears, and the smell of a gun discharged at close range still permeated his nostrils. The irony that he dodged the bullet only to be stabbed in the back wasn't lost on him.

Bloody thickhead. Payne had plunged head-first through the windshield after removing his helmet. That should have knocked him out for more than a few minutes.

If Raven hadn't rescued me, I would have died of blood loss or exposure during the night. Landon owed her his life, and he held tight to the side of the sled to preserve it. At the speed she drove, he would crack his skull if he were thrown off.

Borrowing an RCMP vehicle without permission is a punishable offence, Raven.

As infuriating as she might be, she was also smart, quick-witted, resourceful, and a bloody awesome driver. Becoming infatuated with a witness broke all the rules in the book, but he couldn't deny his fascination or his attraction.

The storm blanketing the forest raged on. He had no idea how she could see or if she even knew where she was going, but Landon didn't care. Dawn was breaking. The longer the storm lasted, the better for them to elude any pursuers.

Raven ventured behind a new stucco house built on a wooded acreage, stopping next to a shed.

"You said no hospital, but you didn't say anything about doctors. This is Caleb's new house. He hasn't moved in yet, but every night, he comes to check on the heating system. Everyone who knows him knows his routine. His visit won't raise any suspicion, and he'll be able to look at your injury." Her ragged breath escaped in a cloud of white mist in the stormy winter air. "I don't know how come I recall his schedule, his phobia of frozen pipes, and his keyless password. This is frustrating. My mind is a scrambled puzzle missing half the pieces."

Her Swiss cheese memory had led them to safety. Weathering the storm in her brother's house would give them time to rest and figure out what to do next.

* * *

Raven hadn't yet had the courage to tell Landon she could hardly hear, but at the rate she asked him to repeat, he would soon grow suspicious. "You want to undress where?"

"Bathroom." Except for his boots, which he removed in the entryway of the basement suite, he had refused to shed anything else. "I'm not leaving a trail of blood on Caleb's new floor and carpet."

"It's not his, it's..." An argument resurfaced in her mind, the words resonating loud and clear. "The basement suite is mine... kind of."

His face scrunched up. "Kind of?"

"Caleb wanted me and Eja to move in with him." Her brother's insistence hadn't matched her tenacity. "I refused to leave the cabin."

"Why?" Leaning against her for support, Landon struggled to walk.

"I couldn't stomach the idea of living in the same house as his girlfriend, not that I told him that." *I hope I didn't share my reasons and hurt Caleb's feelings.* With her cabin no longer standing, Raven might have to beg for shelter.

Once they made it to the bathroom, Landon grabbed the sink with one hand and shifted his weight from her shoulder to the vanity. "Help me take my clothes off."

An inch-long slit punctured his jacket

and work shirt, but the scarf showed no trace of blood. She slowly peeled it from his skin but paused when fresh blood dribbled down. "The scarf is stuck to the wound. You'll start bleeding again if I remove it."

She gazed at his reflection in the mirror, waiting for instructions. His chest expanded, outlining rippling muscles underneath sparse curly hairs. With his clothes on, he looked to be in his late thirties. Without them, he rivaled much younger men.

Landon arched a brow over his darkening brown eyes, and a smile danced on his moving lips.

"Sorry, I..." Heat rushed to her face. She needed to rein in those wayward thoughts before they got her in trouble. "You were saying?"

He encircled her waist. "Take my pants off but leave the scarf on until we're in the shower."

"What?" Stunned by what she understood, she glanced past the bathtub at the frosty glass panels blurring a large ceramic shower. "You want me to go in the corner shower with you?"

"You have a son." With his thumbs, he grazed the sensitive skin along the edge of her sweatpants, cooking up delicious sensations. "I'm sure you washed him hundreds of times. Just think of me as a bigger version of him."

She could only recall Eja in her dreams, and the images her imagination dreamed up at this moment didn't belong to a little boy. "This isn't a game."

"I'm not toying with you, Raven. I can't stand on my own."

"Landon…" These weren't the circumstances under which she had ever imagined undressing him. Her judgment clouded by his phoney kisses, she pressed her palms against his bare chest. His skin was warm to her touch. "You're spiking a fever." Cleaning the wound and removing any foreign objects trapped in it wouldn't stop the infection, but it might slow it down. "Please, don't faint on me."

She lowered his pants, exposing black jersey boxers, similar to the ones she had borrowed from his drawer. However, they hugged much bigger attributes.

A yank on the drawstring of her sweatpants pulled her out of her reverie. She let them slide down her legs, then pulled her sweater over her head. Her clothes pooled at her feet.

"Is that a cuff?" Landon caught her hand. "Why are your fingers taped together?"

Had Caleb not sliced through the chain of the handcuffs, leaving only the one ring around her sore and reddened wrist, Landon's glare would have vaporized the links.

"To make a story short, Tobin arrested me, but I escaped."

"Take the key in my shirt pocket." His

chest heaved under the sharp breaths he took. "You can give me the long version under the water."

While she freed her wrist, he held onto the sink, but his gaze enveloped her half-naked body in a warm and fuzzy cloak. Fear, danger, and the fever riddling his body heightened the attraction she sensed between them.

"Let's get you under the water." The smell of fresh silicone permeated the shower alcove housing a built-in contoured seat and multiple jets. By the time she figured out the controls and water temperature, her red bra and panties were soaked.

Landon sat on the seat in his boxers with his eyes closed.

The scarf blocked the drain. She tossed it on the bathroom floor. "If you were to tell me that you and I were lovers before I lost my memory, or that you fathered my son, it would make this moment less awkward."

Battered by the warm water, his face displayed a myriad of emotions. "Raven—"

On second thought, she pressed a finger on his lips. Now wasn't the best time to deal with her past. "Stay still. While I make you presentable, you can listen to what happened when Tobin broke into your house."

Bar soaps and shampoo bottles were lined up on the shelf next to his shoulder. Her brother had readied the bathroom. She hoped he had also stocked the cupboard with towels.

While she gently scrubbed his cuts and scratches, she recounted Tobin's visit. Landon flinched on many occasions. If he said anything, she didn't catch it. Once she finished with his head and front upper body, she moved to his back. The blood flow had trickled down.

"I was Tobin's bargaining chip." By keeping Landon focused on Tobin, she hoped to divert his attention from the pain she undoubtedly caused while examining his injury. "He wanted to trade me for the paternity test, but not before I begged him for his silence. He'd apparently propositioned me in the past and hadn't handled rejection well." A frayed substance had penetrated the wound. "There's something stuck in your back. It needs to come out." She painstakingly extracted a shred of fabric. "It was a piece of your shirt… I think." Relieved neither of them fainted, she kneeled and leaned her head against his good shoulder. "I'm no doctor. Let's never do this again."

Landon ran his hand into her hair, cupping the side of her head. When she looked up, her lips grazed his cheek.

The steam of the shower had collaborated with the fever to paint a rosy glow over his body.

"Don't move. I'll get something to dry you off." She left the water running down his back so it kept rinsing the wound while she searched the cupboards.

Among the towels piled by sizes and colours were two yellow rubber duckies, a folded pink bathrobe, a hairdryer, and a well-stocked first aid kit.

Her brother hadn't taken no for an answer.

* * *

Something soft grazed Landon's shoulder, rousing him from a nightmarish slumber. Eager to escape the faceless shadows looming over bloody victims, he focused on the fuzzy sensations. As the darkness receded from his mind, throbbing aches returned with a vengeance.

Asleep or awake, there's just no reprieve from pain. He needed more of those pills that Raven had given him.

The ceiling of the bedroom was painted sunny yellow, the bright colour compensating for the dim light coming through the narrow basement windows.

Hazy scenes of their shower flashed in his mind. Riddled with fever, he had flirted with her. He groaned inwardly. *Bloody hell, what were you thinking?*

The woman couldn't remember her son. Alluding to a future together until her past caught up with her had been insensitive.

Something brushed his bare shoulder.

A smile sneaked past his guard, stirring that bloody longing in his heart again.

Lying sideways in bed, a fluffy pillow supporting his injured side, he marvelled at the woman asleep next to him over the comforter. Her hair and the sleeve of her downy pink robe caressed his skin.

Bloody hell, the fever also fried my brain.

Raven stirred, her hand traveling along the edge of the comforter to his chest. Careful to avoid her broken finger, he stroked her thumb. A reddened streak marked her wrist where the cuff had rubbed her skin. Tobin preyed on innocent victims and abused his power and authority. He was a disgrace worthy of a holding cell.

"Who am I, Landon?"

Startled by the soft-spoken question, he shifted his head to meet her gaze.

"Except for Eja, I told you everything I know about you." Her fingers twitched under his touch. "You love your son more than anything in this world. I was afraid it would break your heart not to be able to remember him. I meant to protect you, not hurt you."

Tears pooled in her eyes. "Thank you, and your father, for protecting my son."

"Don't thank me," Landon quipped. "Knowing my dad, he's spoiling Eja rotten, and not feeding him any green vegetables."

Her soft laughter rose between them only to trickle to a sudden stop. "In the shower, when I asked about you, me, and

Eja, I... it wasn't a rhetorical question, but I was afraid of the answer."

The answer scared him, too, but Landon couldn't deny his feelings. "We aren't lovers and Eja isn't my son, but I'd be lying if I said I wasn't attached to him, or to you."

She stared at him like he had grown two heads, when in fact he lost the only one he had. "Does... does Old Raven know you're in love with her?"

"Old Raven?" That split personality answer showed no insight into her feelings toward him. "Not sure. Things were complicated between us."

New Raven's expression remained guarded. "Who's Eja's father? Is he around?"

"As far as I know, you raised Eja alone. You never told anyone about his father, not even Caleb." Landon caressed her cheek. "He's your son, Raven. That's all that matters to me."

Her breathing quickened. "Tobin said the paternity test was for Eja. He said I had an affair with Gage Harrison. You wrote I was a hooker like my mother... I'm not sure I want to be that, Raven."

"Tobin is the one who wrote that report on you, but I don't trust him or his sources." Landon regretted not destroying the report. "Just because Harrison cared about you and your son doesn't mean he had a secret agenda. Not all men are like Tobin. I'm thinking he may have wanted to cast a shadow on your reputation so the threats against you wouldn't be investigated. Your mother and Caleb's were indeed prostitutes, but his grandfather saved both of you from that life. You're a social worker, Raven. You help children. I haven't looked into your alleged arrest in that motel, but charges weren't filed for a reason."

She released a long puff of air that tickled his skin. "Not remembering my son makes me feel like a bad mother, and not remembering his father makes me feel like a hooker. Not sure which one is worse."

The comparison wasn't funny, but it didn't stop chuckles from bubbling inside his belly. Her ability to take revelations in stride and quickly adapt to new situations was remarkable.

"There is something else you need to know about Eja. He was hiding in his treehouse when Harrison was ambushed by his killers. Eja witnessed his vicious beating, and the trauma stole his voice. He hasn't spoken since November."

"No..." Shaken like an autumn leaf, Raven buried her head against his shoulder.

The wind howled outside the window. Amid the storm, warm tears dribbled down his neck.

* * *

Raven felt her son's suffering as

accurately and painfully as if she had witnessed the beating, and when she looked at Landon, the same pain was reflected on his battered face.

It frightened her to realize that he had bonded with her son and that she had fallen in love with him. If her old self harboured different feelings toward Landon, Raven couldn't fathom how she would reconcile her past with her present, or her future.

Landon brought her hand to his lips, then abruptly dropped it to reach for the gun resting on the night table, only to freeze. "Doc?"

"Who?" Her gaze followed his gaze. "Caleb?"

Her brother stood in the doorway of the bedroom, an enigmatic expression glued to his face. "Someone donated blood in the bathroom. You and Steele are in bed. You've been crying, and I still don't see Eja. Did something happen to him?"

"Eja is safe with Landon's father." Once she was reunited with Eja, she would get him the professional help he needed to cope with the trauma. "Someone stabbed him."

Her brother frowned at them. "Eja got stabbed?"

"Not Eja, Doc. Me, in the back." Landon pushed the sheet down to his waist and rolled, exposing his injury. "Raven cleaned the wound and stopped the bleeding, but I'm running a fever."

"I'll get my bag from the Hummer."

Caleb returned moments later with his medical bag.

While he tended to Landon's wound, Raven watched their conversation from the opposite side of the bed.

"You're lucky, Steele. The knife scratched the shoulder blade without breaking any bone or cutting any major blood vessels. Damage is minimal, though it probably felt like someone fired up a blowtorch inside your shoulder." Caleb's analogy triggered phantom pain all the way down to Raven's toes.

"Yeah..." Landon took her hand into his. "I blacked out for a few minutes."

"I can believe that." Caleb applied some ointment and a fresh bandage. "There's no foreign material in the wound, and for the most part, the bleeding has stopped. I disinfected it, but at this point, I'd rather not stitch it. Keep it clean and change the dressing three times a day. I'm leaving you a tube of ointment, some dressings, and a few samples of antibiotics and painkillers. Antibiotic, take one pill four times a day until I tell you to stop. Painkiller, take as needed but don't exceed six pills a day. I'll go home and bring you some food."

"It's too dangerous, Doc." As Landon rolled back onto the mattress, a grimace briefly twisted his face. "If someone sees you brave the storm twice in the same evening to check your new house, you'll raise suspicion. Don't come back until your regular time tomorrow evening."

"You lost blood." Caleb frowned. "And you both need to eat."

"We'll be fine, Caleb." Raven had seen boxes of granola bars under the seat of Landon's snowmobile when she looked for a flashlight. It wasn't a feast, but it would be enough to sustain them until tomorrow. "Honest. How's Rusty?"

"I took her to the vet. She has a gash under her eye, a broken jaw, and a few fractured ribs. The vet performed surgery this afternoon. Rusty won't be chewing anything for a while, but he's confident she'll make a full recovery." Her brother bent to clasp his bag. "In the meantime, she'll be on a special soft diet." His phone fell from his shirt pocket onto the bed.

"That's good news." Raven picked up his phone. "Do you have any pictures of Eja on it?"

Caleb's eyes lit up. "Of course I keep pics of my nephew. What kind of question is that? You also know my password."

"I do?" With her index finger, Raven skimmed over the numbers on the screen, and to her amazement, a pattern emerged. She traced it and the home screen appeared, but she had no idea which numbers she touched. *My fingers are better at remembering than my mind.*

As she flipped through the photos, tears pooled in her eyes. Eja looked cuter and more mischievous than she pictured him in her dreams. Seeing him exacerbated the longing in her heart. Still, she kept looking.

An unexpectedly disturbing photo prompted Raven to pause. In it, a blonde woman
lay face down in the snow. An icicle poked from her neck, and she wore nothing more than a magenta bathrobe and a pair of high-heeled sandals.

Raven showed the photo to her brother. "Who is she?"

"A stripper who was found dead behind The Polar Skin." Her brother pocketed his phone. "I'm sorry you stumbled onto the crime scene photo."

"No, it's..." Images of girls lying broken in the snow flashed in Raven's mind. Their faces sailed past her eyes, and their names, entrenched deep in her memory, soared to the surface. *Jessica, Ashley, Brittany, Alba...*

Assailed by a wave of nausea, Raven hugged her chest and closed her eyes. The girls' names spoke of shattered innocence and lost lives.

A teenage girl found behind a dumpster had triggered the investigation that changed Raven's life. She had infiltrated the trafficking ring to rescue them. Gramp's illness had given her an excuse to come home and—

Eja... The sweet memories of her son filled the void in Raven's heart.

* * *

Landon watched Raven's transformation with guarded hope.

An aura of contentment descended upon her, contrasting with the tears streaming down her cheeks. She smiled, a beautiful, peaceful smile that abruptly froze on her face.

"I suffer from hearing loss? No wonder I can't hear. It can't be right. It must be a mistake. We have to—" Her gaze settled on her brother. "Caleb, we need your help. Now."

With the bloody fever hindering his ability to think clearly, Landon was relieved to see that Caleb appeared just as baffled as he was. "You do?"

"Yes." Her excitement was palpable. "The other night, Alessi stole a paternity test from Tobin's desk, who had snatched it from Gage's desk after he died. We need a copy of the results."

Her brother couldn't have looked more stunned had he caught them having sex. "Tobin took a paternity test?"

"Yes... no." A low growl rumbled in her throat. "Gage is the one who took the test. There aren't that many labs, Caleb. You deal with all of them. You—"

"Those results are confidential." From the edge of the bed, Caleb looked back and forth between them. "Even if I could find the lab that Harrison contacted, trying to access the results is illegal and unethical."

In normal times, Landon would commend the doctor's integrity, but that test held too much significance to too many people. Something had to be amiss. "You need to try, Doc. If you're caught, I'll say I forced you to cooperate. Your neck won't be the one on the chopping block."

Caleb straightened up to his full height. "I'll find a way to get the result. Anything else?"

"The guy who stabbed me had an accomplice." The gunshot resonated in Landon's mind. "Could you quietly inquire if anyone required medical attention following a gunshot?"

"A hardened criminal named Nash Payne and his buddy Jerry Mercer showed up at my clinic before the crack of dawn. According to them, they got injured shooting beer bottles, not that I believed them." A vein pulsed erratically on Caleb's neck. "Payne sustained facial lacerations after a bottle allegedly exploded. If he's the one who stabbed you, you're lucky to be alive. Mercer suffered a gunshot wound to the thigh after a bullet allegedly ricocheted. The bullet had already been removed. I patched them up and sent them home."

Their injuries were consistent with the fight that almost cost Landon his life. "Payne landed headfirst in his snowmobile windshield, and Mercer shot himself with my gun. I know Payne belongs in jail, but what can you tell me about Mercer?"

"Mercer is younger than Payne. He dated Alessi, Payne's niece, before she married Gage Harrison." The doctor sighed. "I got the feeling it was a struggle for Gage Harrison to see his wife hang out with her uncle and ex-boyfriend considering they stood on the opposite side of the law. Anyway, I'll try my best to get the information you want. Now rest, both of you. I'll see you tomorrow night."

* * *

Raven's past had caught up with her.

Venturing outside in the storm to fetch food had helped clear her head. Still, she was no closer to making sense of it, so she paced the bedroom to jog her thoughts.

"In the weeks leading to his disappearance, Gage often stopped by the cabin to reminisce about Gramp's case." It had hurt to relive that fateful winter, to see him play with Eja. "In hindsight, it was obvious he'd harboured doubts about his killers. I should have paid more attention to what he told me." She paused at the foot of the bed and stared at the officer propped against the pillows. "You suspected Gage's death wasn't accidental, didn't you? May I ask why? And why didn't you trust Beck and

240

Tobin with your findings?"

"Why don't you sit?" Landon patted the mattress until she joined him. "A week before Gage disappeared, he showed a fellow Mountie the evidence exonerating the two teenagers accused of killing an elderly man. After Gage was found dead, the fellow Mountie contacted my boss with the information. The fellow Mountie believed in Gage's integrity, so much so that my boss began to suspect a cover-up."

Up until his disappearance, Gage had been nothing but a decent officer. When the allegations of sordid behaviour surfaced, Raven should have known better than to take them at face value. It pained her that she doubted him.

"Over the years, I..." A smile cracked Landon's face. "I gained the reputation of being somewhat of a rogue officer. I get the job done, and I don't break any rules, but I tend to interpret them rather loosely. According to my boss, that made me the perfect officer to investigate Gage's death."

"You're undercover?" Despite her familiarity with undercover operations, it never crossed her mind that Landon had been posted here on purpose. She had to give it to him, he played the role to perfection. "Is Landon Steele your real name?"

"Yeah, but my boss fabricated charges against me so Beck and Tobin wouldn't see me as a threat. She told me to trust no one."

And yet, you're trusting me. "Do you

have to kill me now that I know the truth?"

Tremors shook Landon's chest. "Don't make me laugh. It hurts."

Raven had fallen in love with the man he pretended to be, and she loved the man he really was. The killers were not taking that future away from her. "Tobin is a jerk, but do you really think he or Beck were involved in Gage's death?"

"After Noel Foley was arrested on November 10th, someone tampered with his archived criminal record and erased it from the online database. Only four officers accessed both systems between then and now. Mathis, Edwards, Tobin, and Beck." Landon sank into his pillow. "For reasons I can't share, Tobin and Beck are the only viable suspects."

Someone had ruled out Mathis and Edwards, undoubtedly for excellent reasons, but Raven's suspicious mind instantly labelled one of them the *fellow Mountie.*

"If Gage was murdered because he was about to exonerate the teenagers accused of killing Gramp, why would Tobin or Beck go along with the cover-up and risk their careers? They weren't here when Gramp died. It wouldn't have affected them."

"It would if the killers bribed or blackmailed them. Tobin and Beck may harbour more than a few dark secrets worth killing for." Landon stared at her with a quizzical expression. "What are you doing?"

"I can't sleep with my clothes on." She

tossed her sweater on the floor, then wiggled out of the sweatpants. "Stop grinning like an idiot. You're in no shape to act on what you're thinking. And I am not a hooker."

His eyes shone a darker, richer shade of brown. "I was just thinking how beautiful you look in red."

"Yeah… right…" Amused, she snuggled against him. It had been too many years since someone held her in his arms. She missed the intimacy, the wonderful feeling of loving and being loved in return. "When Old Raven first met you, she knew deep down you were trustworthy, but she was scared to open up and get hurt again." The gentle caress he bestowed on her back encouraged her to continue. "When Fate met you, she sensed she could trust you. Unlike Old Raven, she wasn't shackled with the heartache and betrayal of the past. A part of me envies that Fate was free to fall in love with you. She wanted to tell you, but she was afraid Old Raven wouldn't feel the same way." Reconciling her two personalities felt liberating. "We both love you, Landon, but I'm ashamed to say it took me longer to realize it."

Laughter rippled through his chest.

"You're messing up my pillow, Steele. Stop laughing and turn the light off."

He brushed a kiss on her forehead and the room went dark.

Chapter 14

Seated at the edge of the bed, Landon stretched his stiff, achy shoulder, gradually relaxing the muscles.

Raven had left the confines of his arms and grown more agitated as the day progressed. The brand-new blue carpet had started showing signs of wear and tear where she paced the room in her bare feet.

"Where are you, Caleb? It will be dark soon." The silence bathing the room amplified her words. "If I turn the lamp on, the light will filter around the blinds. Now that the storm is over, anyone riding along the edge of the forest will see it."

In the dark, Raven couldn't hear, but there was always the bathroom. It had no window, only a door facing the hallway. Landon wouldn't mind sharing another shower with her, but the risk of being interrupted by her brother drowned that idea.

"Why the quizzical look, Landon?" Her light brown skin offered a lovely contrast to the pink downy bathrobe enveloping her body. "Was I talking to myself out loud?"

"It was more like a whisper." *A melodious whisper.* "I just heard the door. Caleb is here."

The doctor walked into the bedroom and checked the blinds. "I'm here. You can turn the light on now. I don't want Raven to miss anything."

She sat on the bed and tapped the lamp. Light flooded the room, chasing the shadows away. "You found something?"

"Of course I did. A few techs owed me favours, and I lucked out, but first, let me satisfy Steele's curiosity regarding Jerry Mercer." Her brother tossed a calendar on the bed. "October Bad Boy."

Landon flipped through the months of the charity calendar, stopping on October. "That's Mercer?" His suspect stood on the ice with nothing more than his skates, a helmet, a stick, and a jockstrap. *A different kind of picture looms in your future, Mercer. A nice, clean mug shot.*

"I... I remember that guy..." Raven snatched the calendar and pointed at Mercer's face. "He was at the arena, coming out of the dressing room... I was thinking about riding back into the forest to revisit the place where Gramp was killed. That guy stared at me with such a strange expression. It was the same day you hacked my computer..." The calendar fell onto her lap. "I was thinking out loud. I'm the one who told him I'd be in the forest that afternoon." She expelled a shaky breath. "Mercer and

Payne are the ones who attacked me and killed Gramp. We're just missing the teenager who was with them five years ago."

"They killed Gramp?" The news bleached Caleb's face.

Landon took deep breaths to slow the erratic pounding of his heart. Had he not stopped by her cabin that ill-fated afternoon, Raven would have taken Eja with her. *I almost lost them both that day.* "Put your doctor's mask on, Doc." Losing Caleb to a sudden breakdown wasn't an option, not when the doctor was the only other person whom Landon trusted in this town. "We'll fill you in later. What else do you have for us?"

"When I reported Mercer's gunshot wound, as I'm obligated to do even though I didn't have a bullet, your sergeant said he would investigate it whenever he had time. He was in a terrible mood over your unauthorized absence. Anyway, I went back to the clinic last night. I thought *you* might be interested to know if Mercer's DNA was in the system. I hadn't yet disposed of the gauze with his blood on it, so I sent it to the lab. My friend rushed the results. Mercer wasn't in the system, but his DNA was flagged in Noel Foley's case. Remember the unidentified blood on the rag?" Caleb placed a report on the bed. "This proves it belonged to Mercer."

"So Mercer was more than likely with Noel when he died." Seventy per cent likely if Landon recalled the odds correctly. He had been suspicious of the accidental shooting, but his first suspect would have been Payne, not Mercer. "I guess I'll be reopening this case as well. Anything else, Doc?"

"I got a copy of the paternity test." Caleb handed a folded sheet directly to Raven. "I glanced at the results. Tobin wasn't lying."

Raven's expression became guarded. She unfolded the copy on the bed. "You're both entitled to see this."

Based on the DNA Analysis, the alleged father GAGE HARRISON is excluded as the biological father of the child EB because they do not share sufficient genetic markers. The probability of the stated relationship is indicated below.

Probability Percentage: 0%

Below the probability percentage, a chart contained the list of markers used for comparison. D3S1358, D21S11, D18S51, D7S820...

* * *

Raven skimmed down the chart, searching for one specific marker. Two-thirds of the way down, she found it. The

247

awful confirmation of her fears. Assailed by emotions from all over the spectrum, she closed her eyes.

Gage... There were never any other possibilities, but being correct didn't make her feel right.

Someone caressed her thigh.

She owed Caleb and Landon the truth. One for sticking with her through the past, and the other for wanting to share her future. When she opened her eyes, two sets of dark eyes gazed at her with loving concern. How much they had figured out, she couldn't tell.

"When I found Gramp dead in the forest, I was still reeling from the atrocities I'd witnessed in Halifax. My world collapsed, and I lost my bearings." A void had engulfed her. She had grasped onto Gage, her only link to sanity. "I just needed to be held, to be reassured everything would be all right... That night, Gage stayed with me in the cabin. A few weeks later, in the middle of Gramp's investigation, he showed up with a solemn look on his face. I braced myself for another tragedy. He'd gone out for a drink with Alessi and... and she got pregnant." At the time, Raven had been too numb to feel hurt. "Gage married her a few days later. Their daughter was born two weeks before Eja."

"Are you saying Gage is Eja's father?" Landon exchanged a confused glance with her brother. "Could the results be wrong, Doc? Could they have been altered?"

Her brother shrugged. "Unlikely, but it's

not impossible that someone posing as Harrison requested the test and provided unrelated samples."

Yeah, they'd both missed it. "The results aren't what they appear to be. That's why Alessi stole them. I didn't realize I was pregnant until after Gage married her. I never told him about Eja. When he visited me last fall, he asked lots of questions about the day I found Gramp, but then he made one comment that didn't belong. *Evelyn Britt has brown eyes, not blue like Eja.* It was the first time he used his daughter's full name in front of me. I thought maybe it was his way to tell me he knew about Eja, to acknowledge his son."

Raven placed the results on the bed, facing them. "Look at the AMEL marker, the fifth one from the bottom. Father XY, child XX. The DNA sample came from a female child. EB is Evelyn Britt. Gage had found out his daughter wasn't his, and he told me, but I didn't clue in. Then he disappeared, and I started receiving threats. What if Uncle Payne and ex-boyfriend Mercer wanted me gone, not because I saw Gramp's killers, but because Eja is Gage's child, a living threat to Alessi and her daughter?"

Landon straightened up in bed. "Two things happened around the same time last fall. Gage revisited your grandfather's death and questioned his paternity. While it could be a weird coincidence, it's also possible Gage stumbled onto one truth while searching for the other." A muscle twitched at the base of his neck. "Doc, we must get into town. I have phone calls to make. Is there a place where we could hide? The morgue maybe?"

Caleb waved his hand, his way of catching her attention. "You can stay in my other house."

"What about Annette?" Of all the girls her brother had ever dated, he chose to live with the one incapable of showing discretion or empathy. "Isn't she home?"

"After I brought back Rusty from the vet, she peed on the living room floor. Annette was livid. She gave me a choice. Her or the dog." A bittersweet smile lightened up Caleb's grave expression. "Care to guess which one packed her suitcase?"

* * *

On his first visit, Landon had rung the doorbell. This time, he banged on the door until Tobin answered.

"Steele? What the—"

Landon caught the pathetic excuse for an officer by the front of his undershirt and slammed his back against the wall. The despicable constable crumpled on the floor, and a dent appeared where his head hit the wall.

Dazed from the attack, Tobin struggled

250

to sit. "You're going to jail for this."

Unfazed by the threat, Landon grabbed his colleague's arm and cuffed him to the stove handle. "Your fingerprints are all over the cuffs that chafed Raven's wrists. Judges don't like cops who brutalize and prey on vulnerable women."

His back to the stove, Tobin spat on the floor. "A judge will never believe her words over mine."

"We'll see soon enough, won't we? In the meantime, we'll play twenty questions again." The muscles in Landon's upper back burned from the effort to incapacitate Tobin, and a warm liquid trickled down his shoulder blade. *Bloody injury.* The doctor wouldn't be impressed that the wound was bleeding again. "If I like the answers, I'll leave you alone to contemplate your future."

"Don't go all righteous on me, Steele. You're the one who reported her missing and locked her in your trailer." Tobin's contempt seemed to rise with every word. "For the record, I didn't touch her. You can have her back. She's too wild for me."

"Forget about Raven." In due time, Landon would ensure that Tobin was charged with kidnapping, unlawful confinement, assault, blackmail—and anything else that might crop up. "I want to know about Alessi Harrison. What's your relationship with her?"

Tobin growled. "Who I'm seeing is none of your business."

That answers one question. "Did you get involved with her before or after Gage disappeared?"

"I resent the accusations. I'm not going to let you soil her reputation. Alessi is a decent woman and a wonderful mother." Her name rolled off Tobin's tongue. "We didn't hook up until after his funeral."

Sure. "Let me show you something." Landon pulled the copy of the paternity test from his pocket and held it to Tobin's face. "Look at the AMEL marker, fifth row from the bottom. That's the gender test, Tobin. XX means a girl. EB is Evelyn Britt, not Eja Brook. The pretty widow was screwing other guys, and Gage found out."

"No... Alessi wouldn't lie to me..." The defiance burning in Tobin's eyes slowly faded. "You're trying to trick me."

"A woman with green eyes doesn't end up with a brown-eyed daughter by sleeping with a blue-eyed man. That's basic biology." In the Hummer, Caleb had explained that the probability for such a combination indeed existed, though it would be the exception rather than the rule. "What other *truth* did she feed you? Come on, Tobin. Spit it out."

Tobin leaned his head against the oven window, visibly deflated. "After Harrison hooked up with the stripper, Alessi came to me. She was distraught over the allegations."

When Tobin fell silent, Landon pressed further. "What allegations?"

"That Harrison was having an affair with Raven and fathered her son." Tobin sneered. "Alessi told me that her husband took a paternity test and kept the result somewhere in the office."

Harrison either confronted his wife with the negative result, or she became aware of her husband's suspicions and tracked his activities. Landon squatted in front of his colleague. "Keep going."

"Alessi was ashamed. She didn't want any more proof of his infidelities to be exposed. She begged me to help her." Tobin's voice lost its intensity. "I searched for weeks before I found the report taped under Gage's drawer. I told Alessi that I'd burned it."

"Alessi is the one who stole the result from your desk, Tobin. She played you but didn't trust you any farther than she could throw you." A way for her to gain access to the back door popped into Landon's mind. "You gave her the code to the back door, didn't you? And you erased Noel Foley's arrest report for her. You traded your integrity for sex."

"She loves me... She said so..." The door of the stove opened and closed as Tobin thrashed against it. "I didn't give her any code or erase anything. You're wrong about her..."

The widow didn't guess the code. Too many possible combinations. She got it from someone, but someone blinded by love might not have realized he had given it to her. *I'll give you the benefit of the doubt on the code, Tobin, but not the missing files.* "Foley was a witness. The evidence he gave Gage exonerated the two teenagers accused of killing Raven's grandfather, but someone inside the detachment deleted Foley from the database to protect Nash Payne and his accomplice, Jerry Mercer. Guess who I'm suspecting, *Constable* Tobin?"

"Oh, no. You're not pinning that one on me." Tobin sounded genuinely upset by the accusations. "Whatever Alessi's sleazy uncle did, it had nothing to do with me."

Landon was stunned to hear Tobin share his opinion of Payne. "What do you know about Payne? Do you owe him favours? Does he own you?"

"No, but there are some people in this town you don't want to cross." Tobin leered. "Nobody messes with Alessi's uncle. If you make the mistake of crossing him, or owing him money, you better disappear, or else he'll hunt you down."

Payne may not own you, Tobin, but you're a slave to cowardice. "What about justice? Did you forget what your uniform stands for?"

"Don't talk to me about justice, Steele." Foam came out of Tobin's mouth. "You're no better than me."

"We're done here." Landon cuffed his soon-to-be former colleague's other hand to a drawer handle. "Someone should come to arrest you by morning. In the meantime, do you prefer I gag you with duct tape or a rag?”

* * *

Worried about Landon, Raven paced Caleb's living room in the dark.

After a long phone call with his boss, a woman named Ma'am, Landon had left to pay a visit to Tobin, but that was hours ago.

A shadow wearing her brother's scrubs crept inside the room. Shocked by the tales of deceit and murder she had recounted while Landon was on the phone, Caleb had gone to bed.

He should be asleep, chased by nightmares, not turning the lights on and blinding her. “Mrs. Johnston just called about a razor injury and lots of blood. Will you be okay if I leave you alone?”

“Yes.” Raven hugged a green Afghan to her chest. “Go.”

Her brother slung his winter coat over his back, creating a draft. The disturbance lifted a scrap of paper from the table. It twirled in the air, landing near Raven's bare feet.

She picked it up. The name and phone number written on it surprised her. “Why do you keep Alessi's phone number in your living room near computer books?”

“Who? Oh...” Two shades darker than

255

his burgundy scrubs, Caleb's coat matched the recliner by the television. "Remember the computer courses that Annette was taking? Alessi was her mentor."

The widow had never struck Raven as the techie type. "Alessi knows about computers?"

"She has an advanced computer degree. Annette boasted once that Alessi could hack into any systems, including my medical files." Caleb slipped his gloves on. "I have to go. Try not to worry too much about Steele."

Worrying about him is the price to pay for loving him. Such was the life that Raven was eager to embrace. Duty meant more to him than words or money. She had sensed his disgust toward Beck's or Tobin's possible betrayal. Whether they partook in Gage's actual murder or not was irrelevant. At least one of them broke his oath and deleted the crucial evidence exposing the murder of two innocent teenagers.

Raven suspected Tobin, not only because of his shady character and their past interactions, but also because Gage had once commented on his sergeant's limited computer skills.

Tobin is the only one who had the expertise and opportunity to hack the system from within... Raven stared at the scrap of paper in her hand. *Or is he?*

The widow had sneaked into the detachment once, proving she had the means and opportunity to act alone.

"If Alessi is as skilled as Caleb believes her to be, she could be the one who hacked into the system."

Five years ago, Raven had accepted her fate without asking questions. Tonight, she wanted answers. She scribbled a short note for Landon on the back of the paper and placed it on the kitchen table.

* * *

After urgently summoning his sergeant to the detachment, Landon reviewed Beck's service records while waiting for him to show up.

At fifty-seven years old, Beck has thirty-three years of service under his belt and not a single stain on his service record.

Nothing indicated his sergeant was ever involved in the investigation of Marshall's death or that he ever crossed paths with Harrison until his posting here. He never married or had children, and his financial record showed no red flags.

By all accounts, Beck led a quiet life.

Baffled, Landon closed the screen on his phone and leaned back in the chair facing his sergeant's desk. One of his late mother's old sayings came to mind. *It's the quiet ones you have to look out for.*

"I agree, Mom, but I can't find a single reason why Beck would get involved in the cover-up." If not for the missing evidence, Landon would be inclined to trust his sergeant. "Those bloody files didn't erase themselves. Someone accessed the system."

The front door opened. Seconds later, someone slammed it shut.

Heavy steps resounded in the quiet building, growing louder and closer, until Beck appeared in the doorway of his office, glaring. "You better have a good reason for waking me up in the middle of the night and waiting in my office."

Landon's real boss had dispatched a team to Sprucetown, but reinforcement wasn't scheduled to arrive for another three hours. She had advised him to be patient, or cautious should he decide to confront anyone alone.

I'm yielding your warning, ma'am. I'm being careful. "We have a big problem that may play havoc with your retirement, Sarge, so please sit behind your desk and bear with me while I brief you."

"That looks serious." Looking more puzzled than annoyed, Beck sat with his arms crossed over his unzipped winter jacket. "What happened?"

Surprised by his sergeant's conciliatory tone and attitude, Landon scrutinized him, searching for tell-tale signs of deceit. "Did you know Harrison was murdered?"

Beck dropped his hands onto his lap and stared with wide-open eyes at him. "What do you mean murdered?"

"Murdered, like in killed by Nash Payne and Jerry Mercer. The snowmobile accident was staged. Harrison died shortly after he disappeared, then someone pretending to be him fabricated false evidence to tarnish his reputation and derail the investigation." Landon wasn't sure if he should be relieved or worried to see the colour drain from his sergeant's face. "Weeks prior to his murder, Harrison had unearthed new evidence in the death of Marcel Marshall, Raven's grandfather. The two teenagers who confessed to his killing in a suicide note were framed and killed by the same three individuals who killed Marshall. Nash Payne, Jerry Mercer, and a third unidentified person."

"This is..." His sergeant propped his elbows on his desk. "This is huge, Steele. If Harrison had told me he was investigating his wife's uncle, I would have been suspicious of his disappearance. Payne is a dangerous man, the kind of man who wouldn't hesitate to sell his mother if she crossed him. We may need reinforcement to make the arrest. I take it you have proof to back up these accusations?"

"I have copies, but the original evidence went missing from the filing cabinet and was erased from the online database. Harrison's widow was seen sneaking in by the back door. I suspect she stole the evidence to protect her uncle, but she couldn't have done it without help from the inside." Landon paused a few seconds to let his assertion sink in. "I just had an enlightening chat with Tobin. He's sleeping with her, but he denied given her the entry code or deleting the online files."

"The way Tobin spoke of Harrison... I should have suspected he was having an affair with his widow." Beck's face hardened. "If Tobin played the slightest role in Harrison's death, I will personally drag his sorry arse in jail and throw away the key. Can you prove he deleted the files?"

"Actually, Sarge, I'm not convinced Tobin did. Remember the stern warning you gave me for harassing Alessi Harrison at seven in the morning? Well, I saw someone in uniform leaving her house minutes before I rang her doorbell." Landon met his sergeant's gaze and held it. "I suppose it could have been Tobin, but I also recall seeing your SUV parked a block away from her house that morning. Now I'm wondering if the black widow enticed more than one uniform into doing her bidding."

"You think Alessi and I are..." A grin cracked Beck's face, and he burst into laughter, disconcerting Landon. "I was only protecting the privacy of a grieving widow so I wouldn't have to deal with a complaint. Remember what I told you about *not* rocking the boat? You weren't supposed to sink it either. That morning in question, I was meeting my financial adviser about my retirement. He and I, we... we are thinking of buying a property together. So, no, I wasn't with Alessi, I didn't give her any code, and I certainly didn't delete any—" His sergeant froze mid-sentence and bolted to his feet. "It was her all along."

"Her? Who's her, Sarge?" *If you're thinking about blaming Mathis, or Edwards, please don't. The two officers who came as one to defend Harrison's integrity didn't deserve to be dragged through the mud for an offence they didn't commit.*

"Alessi." A groan escaped Beck's throat as he paced his office. "She's a hacker who works as a consultant to test security systems. Harrison once bragged over a beer that his wife could break into any system. He obviously trusted her, but she chose her uncle over him."

And when she became aware of the paternity test, her allegiance to her husband must have dwindled to a big nothing. Landon's phone rang. At the sight of Caleb's number, he answered. "What is it, Doc?"

"I just found a note on the table. Raven is gone." The panic in her brother's voice engulfed the line. "She went to confront Alessi Harrison."

* * *

The fence surrounding the Harrisons' yard edged a children's playground illuminated by a lamppost. A path in the snow led to a gate left ajar.

Raven added her footsteps to the multitude of boot prints coming and going across the playground.

The back door of Alessi's house opened, and a silhouette stepped onto the deck.

Raven's breath caught in her throat. She crouched behind the upper portion of the slide and waited for Alessi to shoo away her uncle.

As much as Raven wanted to make Payne pay, this wasn't a battle she could win on her own. She trusted Landon to take care of him and Mercer, to right the wrongs in Gramp's murder. Her qualms were with Alessi's lies.

Payne faded in the night, Alessi closed the door, and the light on the deck went off. Still, Raven waited a few minutes before entering the yard.

A child shovel guarded the entrance of a snow fort built near the stairs.

A red shovel, like Eja's. From inside his treehouse, her son had witnessed his father's demise, and the brutal assault had stolen his voice.

The anger that Raven had kept at bay spread unchecked, coiling her insides and brewing revenge. She tiptoed onto the deck. Most people in town never locked their doors. She turned the doorknob and pushed. No resistance.

She inched inside and gazed around the

kitchen.

Hoping to bring Alessi back in the kitchen without waking her daughter, Raven flipped the switch and turned the faucet on.

Light flooded the kitchen and water swirled in a stainless-steel sink. On the counter, dry dishes were stashed in a rack, and an old-fashioned cast-iron pan rested on the stovetop.

Her back to the stove, Raven glanced between two archways, one opening into a living room and the other facing a narrow hallway.

A shadow moved along the hallway, pausing in the archway.

"You!" The look of surprise on Alessi's face morphed into hatred. "You're supposed to be dead."

"Are you mistaking me for my grandfather? The defenceless man killed by your uncle and his friend Jerry five years ago?" Raven modulated her voice, drawing her strength from the pressure of the handle poking the small of her back. "Or your late husband who died in that same forest after he discovered your dirty little secret?"

"Your audacity matches your stupidity, Brook." Alessi's facial expression hardened. "My daughter is asleep. What do you want?"

"When you married Gage, did you know Lyn wasn't his daughter?" *If only I'd known I was pregnant at the time of their gunshot wedding.* Regrets clogged Raven's thoughts, tangling the timeline. Gage hadn't slept with

Alessi until later. *If I didn't know I was expecting, Alessi couldn't have known either unless—* "You were already pregnant when you slept with Gage."

"It's your fault, you know." The widow tightened the belt of her teal bathrobe. "I wouldn't have seduced him if he hadn't been in charge of the investigation, and you hadn't told him you saw three suspects. We'd planned to kill and frame three dropouts, but Jerry only managed to lure two. I had to make sure Gage would dismiss your statement and close the case."

"You..." Assailed by a nauseating feeling, Raven gripped the edge of the oven. *The third killer wasn't a teenager, she was a petite woman.* "You were with them when they killed my grandfather?"

"He caught us stealing a lynx from his trap, called us thieves, and threatened to go to the RCMP. We had to stop him. Uncle Nash was furious that he lost his favourite knife chasing after him, so he made sure your grandfather paid for the trouble he caused." Alessi didn't appear worried that she was confessing to a murder. If anything, the black widow seemed to relish reliving the heinous crime. "He wore nice snowshoes. I wanted to keep them, but Jerry tossed them away. I don't think they were ever found, but I'd like to know how Uncle Nash's knife ended up in Steele's possession?"

Meg had found the evidence that could have sent the trio behind bars, but the irony that she had been too scared and too distrustful of the RCMP to speak up wasn't lost on Raven.

"That's complicated. Why did you start threatening me in the fall?" Raven didn't doubt that Alessi intended to kill her. All Raven could do was buy time until an opportunity to escape presented itself. "You were the one who wrote me those notes, weren't you? The handwriting also matches the teens' suicide note, but you already know that."

"I'm surprised you noticed, though if you'd been smarter, you would have heeded the warning. One of the teens' cousins told Gage that he could prove they were innocent. I couldn't let Gage reopen the investigation. Our marriage was in trouble. He would have shown no mercy toward me." Gage had become expendable the moment Alessi realized she couldn't trust him anymore. "Jerry helped the cousin shoot himself, then Uncle Nash killed Gage, and Jerry destroyed his reputation. His fake moustache fooled everyone. You were the only witness left. I wanted to kill you, but I was afraid your brother would open an inquiry. I wanted the investigation to die, not get a second life. If you'd left town when you had a chance, it would have solved everyone's problem, and your son would still be alive. Now you'll join him." Alessi glanced toward the archway. "Kill her."

From the corner of her eye, Raven

caught movement in the living room. She darted a look and froze.

Jerry stood in the archway, his left thigh wrapped in a large bandage. He pointed a rifle at her, but he wasn't looking at her as much as he was frowning at Alessi. "What did she mean by Lyn isn't his daughter?"

His reaction galvanized Raven. "Gage wasn't Lyn's father. He took a paternity test to prove it, a test that Alessi stole. She only tricked him into thinking he was Lyn's father."

As stock-still as a gargoyle perched on top of a gravestone, Alessi glowered. "Shoot her."

Piercing and dark, Jerry's gaze scorched Raven, reminding her of their encounter at the arena. *He has brown eyes, like Lyn.* "Lyn has brown eyes, Jerry. Your eyes. She's your daughter, your little girl. Alessi took Lyn from you and gave her to Gage." Wishing to create more confusion and discord, Raven threw in calculated guesses while she reached behind her for the cast-iron pan. "Alessi betrayed you, Jerry."

"Babe?" He glanced back and forth between Alessi and her, slowly tipping the rifle downward. "Is that true?"

"Gage remembered running into us in the forest the morning of Marshall's death. He suspected my uncle was involved. I seduced him to save all our necks." Alessi swayed her generous attributes toward him. The provocative move loosened her belt, exposing a creamy cleavage. "The night I invited Gage to my place, I spiked his drink. He passed out on the couch, whispering Brook's name. I had to drag him into my bed. In the morning, he couldn't remember a thing. When I accused him of taking advantage of me, he believed me. He was pathetic."

The words sank in, unraveling Raven's past. Gage had cared about her, but Alessi had orchestrated his betrayal, a betrayal in which he had played no conscious role.

"Gage meant nothing, Jerry." Alessi ran her hand over his arm and onto the butt of the rifle. "You, me, and Lyn, we can finally be a family. You just need to shoot Brook."

A fuchsia object flew across the archway, catching Raven's eye. The object landed out-of-sight behind the wall. Seconds later, a large shadow crawled on the floor, following the trail of the object.

Jerry raised his rifle.

A man in uniform advanced through the archway, his gun drawn. Raven met his gaze. Landon's lips moved. "Duck on three. One, two—"

She threw herself against the fridge, holding the pan alongside her head. A detonation rang in her ears, the air sizzled, vibrations reverberated through the kitchen, and the smell of gunpowder assailed her nostrils. She peeked around the pan.

A chair was broken, and shards of wood littered the kitchen floor. Landon wobbled near the table, rubbing his head.

Slouched against the wall, eyes half-shut, Jerry held a hand to his chest. Blood seeped through his fingers. The widow snatched the rifle from his lap.

Raven flung the pan, aiming at Alessi's arm. It struck her knee, and Alessi fell into a hutch, grimacing in pain. The rifle went airborne.

Gasping in frightful anticipation, Raven recoiled against the refrigerator.

Alessi snagged the rifle by the barrel. Another detonation rocked the kitchen. She collapsed on the floor next to Jerry, who slumped over her, gaping. Landon secured the weapon and then made a call.

Overpowered by the smell of death, Raven struggled to her feet. "Lyn... she can't see..."

"Easy, Raven." Landon wrapped her in his arms. "Sergeant Beck is upstairs with Lyn. He won't let her come into the kitchen." A heartening combination of love and worry radiated from his face. "An ambulance is on its way. Are you alright?"

"Yes..." Tears stung her eyes. "No..." Safe in his loving embrace, Raven wept silently over everything that had been lost—and everything that could have been but never was.

Chapter 15

Flanked by Constable Wesley, the officer assigned to her protection, Raven entered the detachment.

Officers in uniform bustled inside. Amid the chaos, she spotted Landon speaking on the phone in Beck's office. With a motion of his hand, he dismissed Wesley and gestured for her to approach and close the door.

"—the results. Thanks, Doc." Landon hung up and then patted the corner of the desk, the only section clear of paperwork. "I'd prefer you sit on my lap, but that would be inappropriate behaviour. I'd risk being demoted."

"You can't get demoted two days after receiving your promotion to sergeant," she teased. "It would look bad on your service record."

His chest shook. "When I look at all this paperwork, I almost wish I were still a corporal."

In order to catch Gage's killers, Landon had played his role of rogue officer to perfection. Clean-shaven, dressed in a freshly ironed uniform with his sergeant rank, he projected a different image.

Through their ordeal, Raven had glimpsed his true nature and fell in love with him. This afternoon, she saw the man he really was. A respected officer at ease shouldering the responsibility of a daunting investigation.

"I was going to have lunch with you, but the bloody phone kept ringing." He took her hand into his. "Did something happen?"

"No... yes... Wesley dropped a full carton of orange juice on the kitchen floor. It split and made a big splash next to Rusty. She didn't flinch, Landon. She just looked at me, looked at the mess, and started licking the juice. At that moment, I realized I was finally ready to move on, too." Since the shooting, Raven had slept a lot, reminisced a lot more, and cried even more. Through it all, and with Landon's love and support, she had come to terms with her past. While nothing could bring back what she lost, she was now free to cherish it. "Gage isn't a threat to you, Landon, but I did love him. It was just easier to pretend I didn't. It didn't hurt as much."

"You're entitled to keep loving him. It's something Eja will need to hear when we tell him about his first dad." The gentle massage that Landon bestowed on her wrist sent sweet vibrations through her body. "Gage was a good man caught in a bad situation. What Alessi said was true. Their marriage was in trouble. Gage had contacted a lawyer in St. John's on how to handle a divorce and two paternity issues. The lawyer had scheduled a meeting for the following month. When Gage didn't show up, the lawyer crossed him off his list, unaware he'd been murdered. No official paperwork was ever filed, which is why it didn't show up earlier in the investigation."

She twined her fingers with his, nodding. *Gage had deserved better.* "Where did Sergeant Beck disappear to?"

"Lunch with his financial adviser." Glimmers of amusement lit up Landon's eyes. "He's ignoring his phone and staying as far away from the investigation as he can. He doesn't want anything to come between him and his retirement, not that I blame him. At the rate things are going, I'll be buried under paperwork for months to come, and that's not even counting the investigation into the death of Arnold Thomson, Meg's husband. I'm thinking of asking to be officially posted here since the sergeant position is open and no one else is lining up to fill it. Would that sound like a good idea?"

Delighted by the prospect, she held his hand against her chest and smiled. "I'm not sure what it sounds like, but I like it." It would give them time to plan their new life together instead of rushing into the future. "Can I ask why you're reopening the investigation into Meg's husband?"

"According to Thomson's autopsy report, he sported defensive wounds, and unidentified female DNA was found under his fingernail." This evidence explained why his colleagues had suspected Meg. "This morning, I received the results from Meg's DNA. She's not a match, but Alessi Harrison is."

Stumped, Raven dropped his hand. "Are you saying Alessi killed Meg's husband?"

"I'm saying she was there when he was stabbed, but I doubt she acted alone. I'll have to review the evidence and see if we can also place Payne or Mercer at the scene." Landon sighed, leaning back in his chair. "I want to clear Meg's name, but whether I can bring her husband justice is another story."

"Justice is already being served, Landon. Alessi paid for all her crimes with her life, Mercer is handcuffed to a hospital bed, and it's only a matter of time before Payne is arrested. So, thank you for restoring Meg's faith in the Mounties, even if it's in the afterlife." The woman who had saved Raven's life deserved to rest in peace. "When I came in, you said *Thanks, Doc*. Were you talking to Caleb?"

Landon nodded. "He got the unofficial results of the DNA tests. Lyn is Jerry Mercer's daughter."

The results didn't surprise Raven. "How did Caleb get Mercer and Lyn to agree to submit a sample? I thought Mercer was still unconscious following his surgery, and Lyn was already in Ontario with her aunt."

After Alessi was declared dead on arrival, her estranged sister had petitioned the court for full custody of her niece and taken her to Ontario. Despite the feelings that Raven harboured toward her grandfather's killers, she wished the little girl a normal life, away from the shadow of her murderous parents.

"They didn't exactly agree to it." A sly smile flitted across Landon's face. "Caleb used the paternity test results for Lyn and the blood from Jerry's previous gunshot wound for comparison."

"Clever." Her brother and the man she loved shared a complicity that warmed her heart. "Any signs of Payne?"

"No, but when they searched his house, my men recovered bloody long nose pliers from the bathroom and a bullet from the garbage can. The bullet is a match to my gun, the blood on the pliers belongs to Mercer, and the fingerprints on the grip handles to Payne. It looks like Payne is the one who removed the bullet from Mercer's thigh before taking him to Caleb." These discoveries tied Payne and Mercer to Landon's abduction and stabbing. "Payne is a wanted criminal. He won't escape the island."

Officers had been posted at the ferry terminals, the airport, his house, and his workplace, but as long as Payne roamed free, Raven remained a target of his vengeance. "Will Tobin face charges?"

"When the tech examined his phone, she discovered his emails were automatically forwarded to Alessi. That's how Alessi got the codes to the back door, but we may not be able to prove whether Tobin willingly shared them or Alessi hacked his phone." Landon gave Tobin the benefit of the doubt, and Raven didn't blame him even though she wasn't that generous. "Tobin will still face a string of criminal charges related to your abduction. His days in uniform are numbered, and jail looms in his future."

A constable knocked on the door then stepped in. "Sorry to interrupt, Sarge, but the hospital is in lockdown. An attendant was found dead near a back door. Someone matching Payne's description stole his keycard and used it to enter the premises. Constables Karim and Gordon are requesting backup."

*　*　*

Landon was met in the lobby of the hospital by Constable Gordon.

"It unravelled after we called for reinforcement, Sarge. Karim caught Payne in Mercer's room. Payne fired his handgun and struck Karim in the chest. As soon as I heard the shot, I rushed down the corridor. Payne was heading for the staircase. When he turned toward me and raised his gun, I shot him." The constable handed his gun to Landon. "I know you'll have to investigate the shooting, but I stand by my actions. Karim was rushed to the operating room. He's in surgery as we speak. Payne is dead. Mercer is also dead, strangled with his IV line. And the attendant who had gone out the back door to smoke a cigarette was stabbed with... with an unusual weapon. Not sure why Payne didn't shoot him."

"A gunshot would have sounded the alarm, and Payne probably didn't want anyone to be aware he was in the hospital until he could silence his accomplice." Besides, there were no unusual weapons, only weapons of opportunity. "Take me to the attendant first."

"This way, Sarge. It's faster to pass through the building." Gordon led him through a series of corridors, then opened an emergency door leading outside.

Stunned by the eerie sight, Landon paused in the doorway.

The male attendant lay face down in the snow, an icicle protruding from his neck. *Just like Whiskey.*

* * *

Now that the manhunt was over and the three suspects were dead, Landon's investigation had taken a less urgent turn, even though it was far from finished.

He returned to Caleb's house, relishing

the feeling that the woman he loved was finally safe.

Constable Wesley, who played cards in the kitchen with Raven, rose to his feet. "How's Karim, Sarge?"

"Surgery went well. Karim will recover." Though he probably won't appreciate desk duty for the foreseeable future. "You go have a beer with the guys, Wesley. You all deserve a break."

Wesley dropped his cards on the table and bowed his head in Raven's direction. "It was a pleasure, ma'am. I hope you get to see your little boy soon."

"Me too." A radiant smile illuminated Raven's face. "Thank you for protecting me."

After the constable's departure, Landon took his chair and captured her hand. "Ready to start a new life and pick up our little man?"

She leaned forward and caressed his cheek with her free hand. "Yes, but before we embark on a journey together, there is one last thing you need to know about the images haunting me at night."

Landon loved her in the present and he would keep loving her in the future. Whatever happened in the past belonged in the past. "I'm listening."

"When I moved back to Sprucetown, I was protecting a secret. Back when I worked at Child Welfare Services in Halifax, I dealt with stress by going mountain biking. One day, I didn't see the coyote on the trail until

I rounded the curve. I swerved to avoid it and crashed into a bush. I was purple and blue, and dirty."

The glimpse into her former life drew a smile onto his face.

"I went to the hospital. After the doctor examined me, I saw him tell the nurse to call the police. He thought I'd been beaten. A teenage girl lay in the bed next to mine, looking worse than me. She warned me not to squeal, or else Papi would beat me up. Her name was Lindsay. I wanted to ask her more questions, but Papi showed up before I could. When the officers came, I told them about the suspicious Papi."

Hooked on every word, Landon held his breath for confirmation the officers had indeed listened to her suspicions.

"At the time, I wasn't confident they'd taken me seriously. A week later, an officer called. He wanted me to identify Lindsay's body. They'd found her behind a dumpster wearing bright pink underwear and high-heeled sandals. She was the fifth girl in six months to meet the same fate." Her voice dropped to an eerie whisper, sending chills down his spine. "When I saw the picture of the victim on Caleb's phone, she reminded me of Lindsay—and all the others. That's when my past caught up with me."

Landon had realized the picture triggered her memory, but it never occurred to him that she had seen worse atrocities.

"The other four girls had no names. The

police suspected human trafficking, but they had no lead. Papi was an unknown character, one that no one had ever heard of or encountered. Since I could identify him, the police enlisted my help. I began touring the streets at night, accompanied by Perry, the officer posing as my pimp, and his alleged guard dog. His dog used to be on the K9 unit, but Perry had retired her after two years for lack of aggressivity. She was still an awesome tracker and excellent judge of character, so he kept her and never trained another dog. I felt safe with them." Raven's fondness for her handler and his dog shone through. "It took me months to infiltrate the ring. One night, the police raided a cheap motel where I was meeting some girls. Like them, I was taken to the police station, but I wasn't officially arrested or charged. I never thought my fake arrest would one day tarnish my reputation."

Bloody blabbermouth. Landon would like to have a word or two with the person who fed Tobin's flawed information. "I'm sorry, Raven. What happened at the station should have stayed at the station. You should never have become the subject of sordid rumours. Please, tell me the ring was dismantled?"

"Papi and his monsters were arrested. Twenty-seven girls were rescued from locked bedrooms in a filthy duplex." Her gaze wandered above his head. "I was outside helping them to safety when I realized Alba wasn't among them. Perry took his dog and went back inside searching for her. The explosion..." Raven nibbled on her lower lip, drawing a drop of blood. "The explosion came out of nowhere. One moment I was staring at the front door, the next I was lying flat on the ground. Perry was the only officer still in the duplex, the only casualty. Rusty lost a limb but survived. At the time, no one knew Alba was already dead behind a dumpster at the other end of town... Perry went back in for nothing."

"Perry wouldn't have been able to live with himself if Alba had died in the blast and he hadn't looked for her. He died carrying out his duties." Under the same circumstances, Landon would have made the same decision. "Perry would have been happy to know you gave his dog a loving home."

"I couldn't abandon her, Landon. I owed it to Perry to take care of her. Gramp welcomed us with open arms. He was the only one who knew the truth, and he took our secret to his early grave." Her lips trembled. "Rusty was haunted by the deafening sound of the explosion. Every time Tobin visited the cabin, he enjoyed stomping his boot on the floor just to frighten her. I wanted to report him, but I was afraid Beck wouldn't take me seriously."

"Under his dismissive exterior, Beck cared more than he let on, more than he wanted to care so close to retirement."

Landon's enlightening chat with Beck had revealed another facet of his personality. "He wasn't totally oblivious to Tobin's behaviour, but as long as no one was making waves, he was happy to sail away from the rocks. Strangely enough, I wasn't sure I could trust him until I sank his boat." Landon brushed a tender kiss on her wrist. "Talking about boat, are you ready to board the ferry? And build a family with me?"

An enigmatic smile danced on her face. "Yes, for the ferry, but you'll need a unanimous consent for the family."

Understanding dawned on Landon, filling his heart with unconditional love. "Go pack. We'll catch the ferry leaving tonight."

* * *

The cottage where Landon spent most of his holidays lay amid a white blanket of snow on the shore of a frozen lake.

He parked in front of the double garage beside his sister's dark green SUV.

"What if Eja forgot about me?" In the passenger seat, Raven slipped her gloves on and off. "I've never been away from him this long... I've never been away at all."

Watching false insecurities seep through her courageous and resilient nature was both mystifying and mesmerizing. A tender heart fed her wild spirits. Landon couldn't have dreamed of a more incredible woman with whom to share the rest of his life. "A boy never forgets his mother. He will jump into your arms as soon as he sees you."

Pa Steele welcomed them on the front porch. "That's what I call a wonderful surprise." His left sleeve hung loose next to his body while his bent left arm bulged from under his winter coat. "You must be Raven. I'm Patrick, but everyone calls me Pa, or Papa."

His old man gave Raven a huge hug, and she hugged him back. "Nice meeting you, Pa. Landon speaks highly of you and his sister."

"Not sure I deserve his praises, but..." Fresh cuts and bruises marred his father's seasoned face. "But Charlotte sure does."

Suspicious of his father's strange demeanour, Landon eyed him. "Should I ask what happened to your arm and face?"

"Yeah, about that... I broke two ribs and dislocated my shoulder. Not my proudest moment. I'm sure your sister would have chewed my head off if Eja hadn't been there. We were just building a fort behind the garage, but then we needed more snow. There was lots on the roof, so I climbed up. I was almost done shovelling it off when... when I lost my footing." Pa raised his right arm up, but it didn't silence Raven's gasp. "Eja wasn't injured. I landed in his fort, a good three feet away from him. Then the darn shovel hit me in the face. I couldn't move. It scared the living daylights out of

Eja. He just stood over me, staring in shock. That's when I realized he wasn't seeing me. I think he was reliving the beating of your officer. Then all of a sudden, he started crying. We were both in so much pain, Eja more than me, but we've both started to heal."

Eja was supposed to be safe with you, Pa. The accident had rattled his father. Still, it should never have happened in the first place. "Bloody hell, Pa. What possessed you to climb on—"

"Do not chew your father's head, Landon Steele." Raven poked a finger at his chest. "It was an accident. Your father meant Eja no harm."

Pa took Raven's hand into his. "No need to defend me, sweet girl. I deserve a strong admonishment. Now let's go inside. Someone is eager to see you."

* * *

In the vestibule, Landon took Raven's coat from her trembling hand and hooked it on the rack above the sitting bench.

"Eja! Come down, buddy!" Pa Steele winced, yelling. "Someone just arrived."

Bouncy steps reverberated from the staircase.

Raven exhaled a sharp breath. "Was Eja a good listener?"

"He's a way better listener than I am." Pride pumped up Pa's chest. "You raised him well, sweet girl. Just so you know, we would all love to stay in his life."

Eja appeared at the bottom of the stairs, a huge grin stretched across his face. "Mama!" He dashed into his mother's arms. "You have funny hair."

Astounded by Eja's shrill greeting, Landon stared at his father. "His voice... it's back."

His father's glassy eyes shed a light on the circumstances surrounding his little man's recovery. "When you fell, you gave him his voice back." *That's why Charlotte wasn't angry at you.*

"I never meant to traumatize him by falling, but when he started shouting my name..." Pa's loving expression spoke of his attachment to Eja. "He had the most beautiful voice I'd ever heard. Is he still in danger?"

"No, the killers are dead." The nightmare was over, but Landon would still make certain that Eja received professional counseling so he could deal with the memory and grow up emotionally stable. "Eja is safe."

"Well..." His father patted Landon's shoulder. "If you want him to stay safe, you may want to stop his mom from smothering him."

Oblivious of the conversation, Eja struggled to escape Raven's arms. "Mama! You're squeezing me!"

A blaze of unadulterated wonderment burned in her eyes. She fell to her knees releasing him. "Are you... Are you talking?"

Eja bobbed his head with the seriousness of a four-year-old. "Gage told me to hide and stay quiet, but Papa said it was okay to talk, that Gage wouldn't be angry."

"Gage loved you, munchkin. He would never be angry with you." Tears ran down her cheeks. She placed her hands on her son's shoulders, keeping him close. "I see Landon's family took great care of you."

"Papa took me snowshoeing. Uncle Oli got me skates, and I played hockey with Cousins Becca and Penny. Cousin Alex is too little. He stayed with Auntie Charlotte while she made cookies, lots of cookies, and she never gives me peas. Can I keep them? Please?"

Landon swallowed his chuckles. Bringing Eja here had been the best decision of his life.

"I haven't met your auntie, uncle, or cousins yet, but if they're as nice as Papa," Raven glanced at Pa Steele and smiled, "I guess you can keep them."

"Yessss!" A victorious grin spread on Eja's face. "Can I have a dad too? There's one I like a lot."

The request squeezed the air out of Landon's lungs and seemed to cut the circulation in Raven's arms. They fell onto her lap. "You do?"

"Yes, he's..." Eja's voice dropped to an

inaudible whisper, his lips moving for his mother's eyes only.

The promise of a smile swirled on Raven's lips. "If he keeps his promises, and Rusty likes him, I'd say he's a good choice."

Filled with hope and unconditional love, Landon scooped the boy off his feet. "I love you, little man. I love your mom. And I love Rusty. Do you think you could choose me as your new dad?"

His little man wrapped his arms around his neck and gave him a huge hug, sealing the bond between them.

The End

The story behind *Red in the Snow*:

Over the years, I've had the pleasure of working with many wonderful editors. One of them was hearing-impaired. One day, she made a passing comment about how she wished one of her authors would send her a story featuring a strong deaf heroine. Around the same time, one of my readers asked if my next story could take place in her home province.

So, this is how Raven was born and why she lives in Newfoundland.

I hope you enjoyed reading *Red in the Snow* as much as I enjoyed writing it.

J. S. Marlo grew up in Shawinigan, a small French-Canadian town in Québec. She married a young military officer, raised three spirited children, and enjoyed many wonderful postings in different parts of Canada. She isn't sure where time flew, but decades later, she ended up in Alberta with her husband, spoiling four amazing grandchildren and writing Canadian mysteries under the Northern Lights.